THE REEL LIFE OF
ANDREW WILDEN

THE REEL LIFE OF ANDREW WILDEN

A Coming of Age Novel

MIKE BERNARD

Library Tales Publishing

Published by Library Tales Publishing
www.librarytalespublishing.com

ISBN
9798894410289
9798894410937

First Edition, 2026
Printed in the United States of America

Foreword

Once upon a time, there was Blockbuster Video—a kingdom of blue and yellow stores reigning supreme, boasting more than 9,000 locations worldwide and employing nearly 85,000 people. Their presence was inescapable: video rental outlets dotted every city block, small-town Main Street, and suburban strip mall across America. They ruled the Friday night entertainment scene.

In 1989, a new Blockbuster store opened every seventeen hours.

By 2014, they were disappearing faster than free pizza at a school dance.

Chapter 1

Medfield

Medfield is a typical, quiet New England town. It has a church, a diner, a few pizza places, a Cumberland Farms convenience store, a Dunkin' Donuts, and, like most towns across America in 2004, there was a thriving video rental store.

Tucked away at the far end of Main Street, just before the road becomes more residential, sat the Wilden home, a quaint wood-shingled Cape with flowering window boxes and black shutters. It's more than just a house—it's the heart of the community, serving as the local video rental store where families come together to gather their weekend entertainment for movie marathons.

Strolling down Main Street, you can't miss the large bay window out front with a sign that reads:

COMING ATTRACTIONS.

Inside, the Wilden house felt like stepping into a Blockbuster time capsule—and not in the charming, vintage-shop way. Every corner, nook, and cranny overflowed with teetering stacks of VHS tapes, dusty Betamax boxes, and haphazard towers of DVD cases. Movie magic clogged every room, turning the house into less of a home and more of a hoarder's cinematic fever dream.

At the kitchen table sat six-year-old Andrew Wilden munching on his breakfast, his wide brown eyes glued to the flickering images dancing across the TV screen.

Suddenly, his father, James, burst into the room, his infectious energy palpable even at this early hour. Dressed in a white smock and bow tie, he looked more like a mad scientist than the friendly neighborhood video store owner.

Ding! An egg timer went off on the stove.

"Get her. She's givin' out wings!" Mr. Wilden's voice rang out with infectious cheer as he gave his son a wink.

"It's A Wonderful Life!" Andrew shouted.

"Very good, son," Mr. Wilden replied, giving his son an affectionate pat on the head. "Wasn't that good, honey?" he asked his wife, Allison.

But she didn't answer.

Allison Wilden stood at the kitchen sink, absentmindedly stirring eggs in a bowl. Her face was a carefully wound mask, a shadow of sadness dimming her eyes as she clung to the motions of a normal morning. Each slow, rhythmic turn of the spoon felt like an effort at composure.

Across the kitchen, Mr. Wilden bustled about in his usual whirlwind of energy, his quirky charm practically spilling into every corner of the room. He hummed an off-key tune, blissfully unaware of the quiet storm gathering behind his wife's guarded expression.

"Well, in case I don't see ya, good afternoon, good evening, and good night!"

Mr. Wilden leaned in to kiss his wife on the cheek, but she didn't react, lost in her own thoughts.

Andrew's voice cut through the quiet, bringing a smile to his father's face.

"Jim Carrey. *The Truman Show*."

"That's my boy." Mr. Wilden beamed at his son with pride.

"Give me another one, Dad," Andrew eagerly requested, his eyes bright with excitement.

Mr. Wilden furrowed his brow, trying to come up with a challenge for his movie-savvy son. *"Okay, um… 'Don't mess with the bull, young man. You'll get the horns.'"*

"Awe, that's an easy one." Andrew quickly responded. *"The Breakfast Club."*

"Bing!" Mr. Wilden cheered, impressed by his son's knowledge.

"And that's Ned Ryerson from *Groundhog Day*," young Andrew added with a grin, showcasing his deep understanding of movie trivia.

"You're getting too good at this game." Mr. Wilden chuckled, snagging a bite of Andrew's toast before hurrying off to open the store for the day.

As Andrew finished his breakfast, his attention remained glued to the screen, lost in the movie playing on the TV. Meanwhile, his mother continued to stare out the window, her thoughts drifting far away from the Wilden kitchen and the video store and Main Street and Medfield.

~

THE DOOR SWUNG OPEN, and the familiar jingle of bells announced the arrival of eager customers hurrying into the bustling store.

Inside, shelves were stacked high with VHS tapes and plastic DVD cases, each holding the promise of cinematic adventure and escape. Movie posters lined the walls: *Jaws. Apocalypse Now. Pulp Fiction. Rocky. Star Wars.*

A larger-than-life cardboard cutout of *Spider-Man* stood tall beside Arnold Schwarzenegger's *Terminator.*

This was where James Wilden was in his element, his face beaming as he rang up orders and offered movie suggestions to customers preparing for their weekend of entertainment.

Young Andrew meandered his way up and down the aisles, his fingers skimming slowly over each movie title with care. *Romance. Drama. Action. Adventure. Science Fiction.* The possibilities stretched out endlessly, all tucked inside the cozy confines of his small wood-shingled home.

Andrew's head snapped up at the sound of children's laughter cutting through the quiet hum of the store. In an instant, he was at the front bay window, pushing the curtain aside just enough to peer out. A knot coiled in his stomach as he watched them pass—a blur of bright backpacks and mud-streaked jeans, their voices ringing with a freedom he could only dream of.

They were on their way home from school, swapping stories of dodgeball, pop quizzes, and cold, rubbery cafeteria pizza—blissfully unaware of the world beyond their bubble.

Behind him, Allison Wilden set a gentle hand on her son's shoulder. She leaned close, whispering something meant to soothe. Andrew only nodded, silent, his eyes still locked on the carefree kids drifting down the street.

~

MEDFIELD - 10 YEARS LATER

James Wilden was practically a ghost in his own store. The place felt less like a video rental joint and more like a time capsule, frozen somewhere in the early 2000s. In just ten short years, technology—and life itself—had passed him by. Dust motes drifted in the weak sunlight filtering through the front bay window, glimmering over shelves crammed with VHS tapes and DVDs.

James looked just as misplaced as his store: a worn tweed jacket hanging from his shoulders, spectacles perched on his nose, as if he'd wandered out of a history book. Even the air smelled dated—a mix of stale paper and the plasticky tang of a thousand movie cases.

Then the jingle above the door shattered the silence, loud and sharp, announcing the arrival of exactly one customer.

"Well, hello, Michele." Mr. Wilden greeted her, mustering up a semblance of his old cheerfulness. "Haven't seen you here in a while."

"Hi, Mr. Wilden. Yeah, I've been away at school," Michele replied.

His eyes went to her black-and-gray Providence College sweatshirt. "College? My goodness, where has the time gone? Why, just yesterday you were a little girl renting all my *Disney Princess* movies."

"I know, right?" Michele responded, a wistful smile tugging at her lips. She reached down, placed a plastic bag on the counter, and a collection of VHS cassettes spilled out.

"We were cleaning out my room, and I found these. I don't know why we have them; we don't even own a VCR anymore. Sorry. How much do I owe you?"

"Did you enjoy them?" Mr. Wilden inquired, a kind, forced smile toasting his face.

"I guess."

"How did they make you feel?"

"I…I don't remember," Michele replied, confused.

"Maybe there was a line or two that made you smile? Made you think? Brought you to some kind of emotion? Movies can do that, you know. They can hit you right in the heart and never leave. That's my payment."

He smiled at her, then turned to the shelf behind him, sagging from the weight of DVDs and VHS tapes.

"Now, if you liked this, let me show you another one of his films. Lots of romance and some of the wittiest dialogue you could ever…"

But Michele was already heading for the exit.

"No, thank you, Mr. Wilden. I'll… I'll just download it on Netflix or something."

And just like that, she was gone.

James Wilden stood by the window of his shop, pulling back the curtain to silently watch the world rush past. Every head was bent, every face bathed in the cold, white glow of a phone screen. No one looked up. No one noticed the faded COMING ATTRACTIONS still etched in the glass, a ghost of the vibrant letters it once held. No one saw the shop itself, its once-bright paint peeling into neglect.

And no one—not a single passerby—saw the fear gnawing at James's gut, or the heavy sadness carved deep into the cracks and lines of his weathered face. He was invisible. A relic in a world that had moved on. As outdated as the tapes and DVDs gathering dust in his store.

JAMES WILDEN STOOD BESIDE A TALL, institutional-grey AV cart, its metal shelves sagging under the weight of well-worn VHS tapes. Atop it sat a bulky black VCR, a relic from another age. Its buttons were yellowed and sticky, their labels rubbed smooth by years of pressing play, stop, and rewind. Dust clung to its vents, and the small digital clock on its face glowed a stubborn 12:00—forever blinking, a monument to its age and forgotten purpose.

In one hand, James held a long wooden pointer; in the other, a battered black remote. He addressed the lone pupil before him as though presiding over a classroom from another century.

"All right, class, settle in. Now, let's see what we have today. Ooh, History," he exclaimed, pulling out a VHS tape labeled *The History of the World*. He read from the sleeve with enthusiasm: "Mel Brooks' comic genius is unleashed in spades in this episodic spoof of history's seminal moments."

The "class" had an audience of one: fifteen-year-old Andrew Wilden. He'd grown into a lanky, handsome teenager, with a mop of wavy hair and heavy-lidded brown eyes. His long legs were folded awkwardly beneath an old elementary school chair, its hard plastic biting into his thighs—a constant reminder of how much he'd outgrown this room, this ritual.

He spoke carefully, timidly, as if every word had to be weighed before it left his lips.

"You know, Dad, I was thinking… maybe it's time I take classes at the high school."

"School?" Mr. Wilden replied, his voice rising a bit. "Why? We've covered all the basic curriculum: biology, science, math."

"We watched *Good Will Hunting*," Andrew pointed out.

Mr. Wilden began to recite. "*A troubled genius must come to grips with his childhood demons in order to embrace the possibilities his intellect can provide.*"

"That's not really teaching me math, Dad," Andrew replied, trying his best to navigate the delicate conversation. "Like, for biology, we watched *Happy Feet*."

"*The fascinating story of an Antarctic colony whose rituals of mating…*" Mr. Wilden began, but Andrew interrupted.

"It's about singing, dancing penguins."

"Yes, but they were Emperor penguins, Andrew," Mr. Wilden countered before refocusing his attention and beginning to load the cassette into the VCR. "Don't you remember? We learned how the Emperor penguin attracts a mate by singing a unique 'heartsong.' If the male penguin's heartsong matches the female's song, the two penguins mate. That, my inquisitive son, is the very essence of biology."

"Yeah, but…" Andrew paused and took a deep breath. He knew that the next part of the conversation would broach a difficult topic. "I'm not sure how all this is gonna look on my college applications."

Mr. Wilden stopped what he was doing. He stood up and turned to face his son, his expression clouded with confusion.

"College? Don't be silly, you need to help me and your mother with the store."

Andrew's whole demeanor softened.

"Dad, I... I don't think Mom's coming back."

The words hung heavy in the air between them. Neither spoke for a moment, then—

"She'll be back. You'll see. Nobody leaves a movie halfway through. You want to see how it ends, right?" Mr. Wilden said, his voice tinged with uncertainty, as though he were trying to convince himself more than Andrew. His eyes shifted toward the stenciled bay window as a sense of unease settled over him. "Those people just went to work. Kids just went to school," he muttered quietly.

He awkwardly but tenderly placed a hand on Andrew's shoulder and said, "No, son. We'll... we'll stay here. We'll both stay right here."

With a click, the television screen flickered to life, signaling the beginning of the movie/class. Mr. Wilden glanced at his "pupil" with a mixture of comfort and resolve.

"See, Andrew, everything you need is in the movies," he said, his voice mustering up some of his old enthusiasm.

The glow of the television cast an eerie light over Andrew's concerned face as a knot of dread tightened in his stomach. He stared at the flickering images, but his mind ran on a loop, replaying every strange look, every mumbled word. The realization had been creeping up on him for weeks— subtle at first, easy enough to ignore—but now it was undeniable.

His dad was losing it. Not just sad or stressed, but truly, deeply troubled—adrift in a sea of confusion Andrew had no idea how to navigate.

~

ANDREW STOOD at the kitchen sink, slowly turning eggs in a bowl, mirroring the same sense of sadness and discontent that once plagued his mother. When Allison Wilden left, Andrew was forced to step up to the plate, taking on the responsibilities of maintaining the house. But her departure left a void—a silent ache that lingered with each passing day.

No note. No goodbye. No explanation. Just an empty space where his mother used to be.

Andrew woke up one morning, turned on the TV (like always), and waited for her to come into the kitchen and start breakfast. That was three years ago. Once he saw that her clothes were packed and gone too, Andrew knew it was permanent—something his father refused to believe or even acknowledge.

Maybe she'll be back, like his father believed.

Maybe.

He shook off the heavy thoughts, turned back to his breakfast, and lost himself in the familiar ritual of reciting movie lines. First up: *Groundhog Day*.

"Okay, campers, rise and shine, and don't forget your booties 'cause it's cooooold out there today. It's coooold out there every day."

POOF! A gas burner lit the stove.

Then Chief Brody in *Jaws*.

"You come on down here and chum some of this shhhhh..." Andrew recited as the eggs sizzled on a hot pan.

John Wayne in *The Cowboys*.

"Saddle up. We're burning daylight!" he yelled as he slung a towel over his shoulder.

But the house remained silent.

Andrew turned off the burner, wiped his hands on the towel, and headed upstairs to wake his father.

"Come on, Dad!" he shouted like Simba trying to rouse Mufasa in *The Lion King.* As he climbed each step, he playfully shouted, "Dad! Dad! Dad! Dad! Dad!"

Nothing.

Andrew pushed open the bedroom door, expecting to find his father still asleep. Only this time he didn't quote a movie. There was terror in his voice.

"Dad? Are you OK, Dad?"

James Wilden sat huddled in the corner, gently rocking back and forth, his body trembling with fear, his eyes vacant. He squeezed them shut, wishing he could disappear—wishing the world would stop spinning long enough for him to catch his breath.

CHARLTON MEMORIAL HOSPITAL

Danny Muldoon fidgeted in the hospital hallway. His face, still rounded with boyish softness, made him look younger than his thirty-six years—super annoying when he was trying to be taken seriously. He'd only been on the Medfield police force a few years, and every day felt like an audition he was failing.

Especially with Frank Kobolowski as his partner.

Frank was a fixture of the Medfield police force, his paunch spilling over his belt, his military-style haircut signaling a no-nonsense, old-school approach. His eyes—always narrowed in suspicion or boredom—swept the sterile hallway, missing nothing. Meanwhile, Danny, still buzzing with a rookie's restless enthusiasm, shifted his weight, eager for whatever came next.

Muldoon reached into his uniform pocket and pulled out a palm-sized notepad, a constant and trusted companion in his line of duty.

"No known relatives. Neighbors say the mother left a few years back," he reported to Frank, his voice tinged with concern.

"You got an address at least, right?" Kobolowski grumbled, adjusting his overworked belt.

Muldoon began to flip through the trusty notepad. "They lived upstairs from the video store off Main Street."

"*COMING ATTRACTIONS?* That place is still open?" Kobolowski's reaction filled the hallway. "Damn, I think I still got a copy of *Top Gun* from there. Late fees are gonna be enormous."

Muldoon couldn't help but smirk. Of course, Kobolowski rented *Top Gun*. It was just the kind of macho movie with noise and guns and planes and reflector sunglasses and military haircuts that Kobolowski loved.

Muldoon consulted his notepad (again) and approached Andrew in the waiting room.

"All right, young man. You are…" He scanned the page. "Andrew Wilden. Is that correct?"

Silence.

Muldoon persisted. "So, let's review. We have one male, Caucasian, forty-one years of age, and a reported 10-57."

Kobolowski stepped in, rolling his eyes at Muldoon's awkward attempt to get any information.

"You don't talk to a teenager first thing in the morning, Dan. Hell, the rest of the day's pretty much a wash too. Let me handle this."

He leaned down to meet Andrew eye to eye in a father-to-son kind of way.

"10-57 is a missing person. Wouldn't expect you to know that," Kobolowski addressed Andrew directly, his tone softer. "Do you know where your mom is, son?"

Andrew remained silent, his eyes fixed on the floor.

Kobolowski shook his head. Years on the force hadn't hardened Frank; if anything, they'd softened him—especially when it came to teenagers. He'd seen enough screw-ups, enough misguided rebellions, and enough fear hiding behind defiant eyes to know most kids weren't bad, just lost.

The streets had a way of chewing up the vulnerable, and Frank, a bear of a man with unexpectedly gentle eyes, had made it his mission to be a buffer.

He'd rather talk a kid down from a bad decision than fill out arrest reports, preferring a quiet word and a slice of pizza to the clang of a jail cell. It was an approach that sometimes baffled his fellow officers, but for Frank, watching a teenager walk away with their head held a little higher was reward enough.

Andrew Wilden needed help, and Frank knew just the person. He pulled Muldoon aside.

"You've got a real way with people there, Danny," he said dryly, fishing a card from his pocket. He pressed it into Muldoon's hand. "Here. You're gonna need to call this place."

Muldoon's face suddenly turned pale. It was obvious that he recognized the name.

Really? *Her?*

"Can't… can't you call?" he pleaded.

"All you, big guy. Just be your charming, chatty self," Kobolowski said with a playful whack on the shoulder of his junior partner.

PETERSON HOUSE

The Peterson house is a sprawling Victorian in varying states of mess. Bowls crowd the sink, papers scatter across tables, and piles of books lie in teetering stacks on the floor. It's a living, breathing testament to a family that values passion over tidiness.

A faint scent of old paper and brewing coffee usually lingers in the air, occasionally punctuated by burnt toast or the sharp tang of overdone leftovers from the microwave. Every surface tells a story: a half-finished jigsaw puzzle on the coffee table, sheet music spilling from the piano bench, a forgotten watering can beside a thriving—if slightly overgrown—fern.

It's not a house that's given up; it's a house that's lived in—deeply, joyously, and chaotically.

Three enthusiastic dogs barked and scampered to greet Claire Peterson as she rushed into the kitchen. She was running late—as always. She had half a bagel dangling from her mouth, and she hopped on one foot, struggling to slide into a shoe.

"I gotta run," Claire called out to someone in the other room, her words muffled by the bagel.

Now in her mid-thirties, Claire carried an air of frenzied

indifference that had become her hallmark. Her once neatly styled hair now tumbled in unruly waves around her face, often tangled and in need of a good brush. Her clothes, a mismatched mess of comfort over style, hung loosely on her frame, suggesting someone who had long abandoned the care for appearance that she once possessed. Claire's eyes, once a vibrant shade of green, now looked perpetually tired, shadowed by dark circles from sleepless nights.

Her house mirrored her disarray: books scattered, dishes piled in the sink, and laundry strewn about everywhere. Despite the mess, she navigated through it with a kind of practiced ease, as if the disorder were a map she understood all too perfectly.

Since her husband walked out the door years ago, Claire had built a fortress around her heart. She deflected any mention of romance with a sarcastic remark or a dismissive shrug. Her friends had stopped trying to set her up, knowing it would only be met with resistance. Yet, beneath her *I don't really care* and disheveled exterior, there were fleeting moments when her façade cracked—a wistful glance at an old photograph or a deep sigh when she thought no one was watching.

Claire buried herself in work, wielding it like a massive shield. The world outside? Nope. The messy feelings inside? Double nope. She kept insisting that "love is overrated" and she was "totally fine on her own."

But the truth? Claire was completely lost in her own head —a maze she'd built without realizing it. She longed for a way out but couldn't even see where to begin.

"Sorry about last night," she called out. "I was tired and cranky and, well, sometimes a girl just wants to come home and slip into a bath of wine, ya know?"

Silence filled the air, only broken by the clatter of Claire scurrying around the kitchen.

"That was a joke. Sort of. Okay, so, I gotta go. I'll see you later. There's milk in the fridge; try and make yourself something to eat."

More silence. Claire pressed on.

"This is good, right? *Right?*"

With a final check around the messy kitchen, she hopped out the door, shoe in hand, bagel clutched between her teeth.

MEDFIELD HIGH SCHOOL

Kids shuffled through the halls, lost in their own digital worlds—earbuds in, heads down, thumbs flying over the screens of their latest iPhones and smart tablets. Flat-screen TV monitors hung from the ceiling, vainly attempting to grab the student body's attention with morning announcements, but no one seemed to notice them—or each other.

Three girls gathered around a locker. Those were the *Plastics*, Numbers 1, 2, and 3.

To an outsider, they were indistinguishable from one another. They dressed alike, talked alike, looked alike, and acted alike. They projected an air of royalty—a self-designed social status claiming their place at the top of the high school food chain. They were the "It" group—a place where only the flawless, the coolest, the richest, and the most fashionably elite could survive.

"Oh. My. Gawd," exclaimed Plastic 1. "Did you see what happened on *Real Housewives* last night?"

With too much eye makeup and salon-colored blonde hair, she was a textbook example of high school female perfection, right down to the constant look of disgust.

"Don't. No spoilers," replied Plastic 2, her eyes never leaving her phone.

"Tell her what happened," urged Plastic 3—the shortest, slightly plumpest, and the most eager to please of the three.

"No! Nobody say a thing. Not a word. I downloaded it," snapped Plastic 2, her fingers flying over the touchscreen like a squirrel on caffeine and sugar, darting and tapping away with wild energy.

Finally looking up from her phone, Plastic 1 noticed Molly

Peterson standing beside them, fumbling with her locker. To the *Plastics*, Molly was practically invisible. She wore glasses, her straight brown hair falling in wispy bangs, and dressed in bland, unimaginative clothing.

So plain, in fact, that she somehow stood out among the flashy trio. And Molly—fiercely independent as ever—couldn't care less what those three identical drones thought.

"Don't look at me," Molly said, full of confidence. "I've never seen it." She opened her locker. "We don't have a television," she stated matter-of-factly, with a hint of pride in her voice.

Molly had come to accept her television-less situation. In fact, she was even kind of proud of it in today's *Must See TV* society.

Plastic 2 looked like her head might just spin off her shoulders. Her perfectly plucked eyebrows practically shot to her hairline, revealing her first expression beyond deadpan boredom. It was pure and utter disbelief.

"So, like, you've seen nothing?" asked Plastic 1. "So, like, no *American Idol* or *Vanderpump Rules*?"

"Nope," Molly replied with an air of satisfaction, punctuating the word with a slam of the locker door.

Plastic 3 couldn't be bothered by the whole interaction. She was too busy typing a reply that was undoubtedly the single most important thing in the whole wide world. (For the record, it was a reply ROFL to an earlier LOL, which was a response to a well-timed LMAO… you know, important stuff like that.)

Plastic 1 couldn't wrap her well-coiffed head around the whole thing.

"Wait. So, like, you haven't even seen *The Kardashians?* Like… none of them?!" Her disbelief was palpable.

"Sadly, no," replied Molly, dripping with sarcasm and sort of relishing the moment.

To be clear, Molly Peterson was cool. She had an effortless beauty and a confidence about her that she didn't even realize.

It was a vibe. A nonchalant *I know something you don't* kind of thing.

She wasn't like most other high school girls. She wasn't into flirting or sports or popular trends. It was almost as if she were older and wiser than her fifteen years.

When Molly talked to people, she met their gaze head-on, almost daring them to look away. And when people spoke to her, she listened—like, really, genuinely listened. And cared. It was a rare quality for a fifteen-year-old girl who didn't have a television and didn't follow all the high school norms and trends.

That was part of what made her so intriguing—a cool mystery wrapped in *I-don't-really-give-a-shit-what-you-think-about-my-clothing* kind of confidence.

Plastic 1, clearly the leader—probably because she was the tallest, and her hair was so blonde it almost glowed in the dark—had heard enough from this television-less loser.

"Guys, you have to come over and watch *The Bachelor* tonight. It's the final rose."

"Like, totally," added Plastic 2. She was the kind of girl who pronounced the word with an exaggerated ending—as in, *Like, total-Ē-yah.*

Suddenly, a voice interrupted their conversation.

"Whadd-up, ladies?"

It was Michael Johnson, better known among the halls of Medfield High School as Skype.

Skype was your typical doughy, zitty freshman—always trying way too hard to seem cooler than he was, and desperate to fit in with the crowd. Any crowd. His perpetually slicked-back hair defied gravity in odd places, and his attempts at a casual lean against lockers usually ended in an awkward slide.

He had a habit of adjusting his backpack straps every five seconds, as if bracing for an invisible escape, his nervous energy practically humming. His clothes were always a size too big, like he was trying to hide—or maybe just hoping to grow into them.

He laughed too loudly at jokes he didn't quite get, and his eyes darted around the cafeteria, silently pleading for an invitation to any table.

"You want to be in my Snapchat story?" he asked eagerly, waving his cell phone.

The Plastics barely glanced in his direction, silently questioning how they even let him enter their airspace.

"I'm gonna be famous one day," he declared with confidence. "You can say you knew me when."

Suddenly, his cell phone buzzed. Skype shot the girls a cocky grin as he answered it.

"Probably one of my crew. My boys are always hittin' me up," he boasted, holding the phone to his ear. "Yo. Whadd-up, playah?"

His face crumbled as a voice boomed from the phone.

"Michael, you left your *Romeo and Juliet* book at home. I found it in your room. And why, young man, is your underwear still not picked up? How many times have I told you to put your dirty underwear in the hamper?"

Aw, shit. It was Skype's mom on speakerphone for everyone to hear. He scrambled with his phone, desperately trying to mute the call, turn down the volume, or toss it out a nearby window—anything to make his mom's voice disappear.

"Do you want me to bring your notebook to school, sweetie? Michael? Hello?" Mrs. Johnson's voice echoed through the school hallway, adding to the embarrassment.

"Put your underwear in the hamper, Michael," Plastic 1 mimicked, as the trio laughed and walked away, leaving a trail of attitude, spearmint gum, and expensive perfume.

Skype slumped against the locker, trying to recover from the nightmare. He finally silenced his mom.

"It's okay, Mom," he muttered weakly into the phone. "Yeah. Uh-huh. Love you too. Bye."

He turned to Molly, who was standing at the lockers,

hoping to salvage some dignity but feeling as lost as a drowning man grasping for a rope.

"Hey."

"Hey, Skype… Sorry, I mean Michael," Molly corrected herself.

"That's cool, I'm used to it. My crew calls me Skype now, so…" He trailed off, realizing Molly wasn't impressed by his attempts to be cool. "Can I borrow your Shakespeare notes?" he asked, eager to change the subject. "I really don't need my mother bringing it here and walking the halls calling out my name."

Molly smiled. "Sure, but you'll need to write your own essay. Form your own opinions and ideas. That's the only way you're going to create original thought."

Skype smirked confidently. "I'm saving all my 'original' thoughts to become an internet sensation. YouTube. Snapchat. Instagram. Did you know some dude made five million dollars last year posting videos?"

"I wouldn't know," Molly said dryly. "My mom literally just let me get Facebook."

"Oh yeah?" Skype replied, trying his best to downplay his excitement. "You, um… you can friend me… I mean, if you want."

"Sure. I'll do it later."

"Promise?!" Skype replied, a little too eager.

"Of course," Molly assured him with a genuine smile. Then, reaching into the locker, she handed over her Shakespeare notes. "You'll be my one and only Facebook friend."

"Yeah. Mine too," he muttered, his voice barely above a whisper as he watched her walk away.

A sharp flicker of regret pierced him. He always thought of the perfect thing to say five minutes too late—or the brave thing to do once the moment had already passed. Now all that lingered was the hollow weight of another missed connection with a schoolmate.

DEPARTMENT OF CHILD PROTECTIVE SERVICES

Claire Peterson's tiny office mirrored the chaos of her messy home life. Bulging manila folders and stacks of papers covered every surface, while half-empty Starbucks cups littered her desk.

"She'll totally get to it," she told herself every single day. "For sure, tomorrow." But that was just another lie she'd chosen to believe—a comfort blanket keeping the real, urgent stuff at bay for one more day, one more hour, one more second of not having to face the chaos in her life.

As she rummaged through the clutter, a faint tap sounded at the door.

"On a bit of a search-and-rescue mission here. What's up?" Claire called out without ever looking up.

Officer Muldoon stood nervously in the doorway, clearly uncomfortable. He was as awkward with women as he was with teenagers.

"Sorry to interrupt, ma'am. We have a 10-57. That's a missing person, ma'am. Allison Wilden. There's an ATL..." He fumbled for his trusty notepad, nearly dropping it, and stumbled over his words.

Classic Danny Muldoon when he was nervous.

"And a Caucasian male, forty-one, Mister James Wilden. He's infirmed. Leaving one Andrew John Wilden, fifteen years of age, also Caucasian, to be remanded to the state until we can establish parental support..."

Claire finally stopped her search and looked up. "Stop," she said firmly. "Fifteen? Is that him out there? Andrew, is his name?"

"Yes, ma'am. Andrew. His father was infirmed with an undetermined condition..."

"In English, please, officer," Claire interrupted again, her patience wearing thin.

Muldoon adjusted his tone. "His dad is in the hospital.

Some kind of breakdown. They're not sure how long he'll be there, and we can't find his mother. He has no one… ma'am."

A softness fell over Claire's face as she glanced at the lonely boy sitting outside her office. Poor kid. "Has he been waiting long?"

"No, ma'am. Well, yes, ma'am. We arrived at 0900. Apparently, you were running late," Muldoon informed her.

"Yeah, I hear that a lot," Claire murmured, her mind racing. It was a familiar sting, a reminder of everything she was constantly trying—and failing—to keep up with. "Unfortunately, there's no local foster care available right now. The only housing option we have is in Boston."

Claire and Muldoon exchanged a look, their concern evident. It was clear that moving the lost teenager to the city wasn't a good option. Neither of them wanted Andrew to go. Then, Claire had an idea.

"What did you say your name was, Officer?"

"Muldoon, ma'am. Daniel Muldoon. Actually, you and I —I mean, we—we went to…"

"Are you married, Officer Muldoon?" Claire interrupted again, already formulating a plan. "Do you have kids?"

"No, ma'am," stammered Muldoon, turning three shades of bright red. "I used to live with my mother, but she recently…"

Claire seized the opportunity. "So, you have plenty of room. Perfect. He could stay with you."

"Me? Oh, no, ma'am. I'm not very good with…"

But Claire wasn't listening. Her head was down, rummaging through her messy desk.

"I'll start paperwork for emergency housing. It's Medfield —part of our *Small Town, Small Rules* policy," she said with a kind of wink-wink, nod-nod. "It's only a temporary court order until we find more local foster care or figure out this 10-54 business."

"10-54 is livestock on the highway, ma'am," Muldoon corrected automatically.

"Well, be thankful I'm not asking you to live with a cow then," Claire replied with a smirk. Her eyes softened. "That was a joke, Officer. This is good, *right? Right?*"

"Yes, ma'am. I mean—no, ma'am. Wait… what?" Muldoon was thoroughly confused. He stared at her like a deer caught in headlights, his brain a jumbled mess as he frantically tried to make sense of it all.

"Officer Muldoon?" Claire interrupted his thoughts.

"Ma'am?"

"Bring Andrew in. I'd like to say hello," she instructed him.

"Yes, ma'am." Muldoon left the office—totally bamboozled—then escorted Andrew in.

"Andrew, this is Miss Peterson," Muldoon said, leaning in and then repeating the words louder and slower: "I—said—this—is—Miss—Peterson."

Claire rolled her eyes. "Danny?" she said softly.

Muldoon eagerly looked up, thinking she may have recognized him.

"Ma'am?"

"Go." She pointed toward the hallway and added with a gentle smile, "You two will have plenty of time to get to know each other."

Claire turned her attention to Andrew.

"You wanna tell me what school you're from?"

Andrew remained silent, his gaze fixed on the glasses perched on top of Claire's head—the way they teetered precariously, as if they could fall at any moment.

He wondered, *Does she even know they're there?*

"Not very chatty, huh? That's okay, I'm used to that," Claire said, breaking the silence. "We'll need to get you settled in. Welcome to Medfield High School, home of the Red Raiders—although my mother insists you shouldn't call them that. It's insensitive to Native Americans."

Andrew sat quietly and glanced around at the clutter on Claire's desk: a Rubik's Cube, a small plastic snow globe, what appeared to be a miniature rake with sand. His eyes landed on the posters above Claire's head. One showed a tiny yellow kitten hanging from a tree branch with the words *Hang In There!* below it. Another read *One Day at a Time* in needlepoint.

"I hate those things," Claire said, waving a dismissive hand. "Bumper-sticker philosophy. They came with the office."

He wondered if she really meant it, or if she was just trying to sound cool.

Suddenly, she sat up and shouted, "Aha, found it!" Then, with the half-eaten bagel in her mouth, she exclaimed, *"Go Red Raiders! Yeah!"*

MEDFIELD HIGH SCHOOL

Andrew stood in the bustling school hallway, his eyes wide with a mix of wonder and nervousness as he took in the tumultuous, vibrant energy of Medfield High. Everything felt so new, so colorful, loud, and overwhelming in the best possible way. He had dreamed of going to school—a real school—to have lots of friends, hang out, and do normal stuff like that, but experiencing it firsthand was a whole different story.

The bell rang, and suddenly the hallway exploded with activity. Doors flew open, unleashing a rush of students flooding into the hall like salmon swimming upstream. Claire and Andrew meandered through the maze of bodies as backpacks collided and sneakers squeaked across the tiled floors.

Andrew's heart raced. He did his best to navigate the chaos, his eyes darting to take it all in: lockers slamming shut, colorful posters advertising clubs and events, groups of friends laughing together. It was overwhelming—and utterly wonderful. The promise of a brand-new adventure.

"Wait here," Claire shouted over the noise. "I'll find out where you're supposed to be."

Andrew watched as Claire made her way down the hall, a

blur of motion as she effortlessly wove through the tight packs of students. Her bright personality and sheer determination seemed to deflect anyone bold enough to stand in her path.

He leaned against a locker, trying not to be noticed. Kids hurried past, heads bent over their phones, ignoring him—and each other. A few glanced his way, but there was no hint of friendship in their faces. They were too absorbed in their digital worlds—texting, scrolling Instagram, liking Facebook posts, and watching Snapchat stories.

A voice thundered, "Gooooood Mooooorning, *Red Raiders!*" and suddenly the crowded hallway scattered like someone had just released a swarm of bees, making way for Ricky Sherman and his entourage of Sidekicks.

"Outta the way, losers!" the overgrown bully yelled, planting his feet wide and puffing out his chest, daring anyone to challenge him.

Andrew narrowed his eyes. He recognized this character from every high school movie he'd ever seen: Biff Tannen in *Back to the Future*, Scut Farkus in *A Christmas Story*, Johnny Lawrence in *The Karate Kid*. They were all the same—arrogant, overgrown, testosterone-filled bullies who swaggered around like they owned the place, believing they were the coolest, baddest, toughest dudes around. They were the ones everyone either feared or wanted to be—or at least that's what they thought.

"Ah, what are you doing?" Ricky barked, eyeing Andrew up and down. "You're standing in front of my locker, man. Move!"

"You heard him!" repeated a Sidekick, as if right on cue. "Move!"

Andrew stayed silent, standing motionless.

"Who is this kid?" Ricky asked as he leaned in menacingly close, sounding more annoyed than mad.

The bell rang, signaling the need to hurry off to class—but not before Ricky threw a fake punch in Andrew's direction.

But Andrew didn't flinch.

At all.

In fact, he didn't even blink.

Claire was making her way back down the hall with Andrew's class schedule in her hand.

"The receptionist was just about to shut down her computers—something she reminded me of several times. I don't think she likes her job," Claire said breathlessly, watching Ricky and the Sidekicks slink away.

"Making any friends already? Good for you."

Her eyes skimmed the class assignments in her hand. "So, hmmm, let's see. Vernon Gleason? Really? I can't believe he's still teaching here. I also can't believe he's still alive. Well, anyway… yay for high school. This is good, right? *Right?*"

Claire was doing her best to help sell the situation, but Andrew was too busy taking in all the wonder around him.

Claire ushered Andrew into the classroom and placed a manila folder on the desk.

"Mr. Gleason, this is Andrew Wilden," she announced with authority. "He's a recent transfer to the district."

"Wonderful," snapped the never-cheery Mr. Gleason with an exaggerated eye roll. "More minds, same pay rate."

Every school seemed to have its own version of Vernon Gleason—the classic *power-hungry, know-it-all, hates-his-life* type. His emotions cycled between anger, rage, and bitterness, all fueled by a complete impatience with anyone who crossed his path. His face was almost always a deep shade of red—sometimes even purple—prompting students to wonder if it was psoriasis, rosacea, high blood pressure, or simply a perpetual state of irritation.

"Love the dedication there, Vern," Claire snapped back.

"Two hundred and sixty-three days left 'til retirement. Not counting snow days," he replied with a shit-eatin' grin.

Claire leaned to Andrew and whispered, "He hasn't changed since I had him a hundred years ago."

Andrew wanted to smile but resisted the urge. Head down,

he did his best to avoid eye contact as he slid into an open seat in the front row, wedged between Skype, who was busy doodling his autograph (*Skype. Skype. Skype. Best Wishes, Skype. Have a great summer, Skype. Thanks for watching, Skype*) all over his notebook, and Molly, who was buried in a book—as always.

Trying to look cool and collected, Andrew folded his hands, sat up straight, and stared ahead, channeling the "serious student" vibe he'd seen in so many teen movies.

Claire gave him a reassuring nod as she headed out the door, but not before pointing at Molly. "Keep an eye on her, Andrew. She's *wicked smaht*," she said with a playful wink and an exaggerated, thick Boston accent.

Molly immediately slumped in her seat, wishing she could crawl underneath.

"Homeschooled, huh?" growled Mr. Gleason, flipping through Andrew's folder, then tossing it in the drawer. "Great. Another living-room Einstein. Well, I'll try to be as fascinating as your last teacher."

Ricky faked a cough and shouted, "Loser!"

The entire class erupted in giggles.

Andrew already hated it here.

"Settle down," Gleason addressed the class. "Mister Sherman. Why don't you enlighten us with the homework assignment from last evening?"

The chair squealed loudly against the floor as Ricky sat up, his face a picture of sheer panic. He glared directly at Skype. "Don't you, like, have it on your desk, Mr. Gleason?"

"No, Mister Sherman, *I, like, don't. Am I, like, supposed to?*" he replied, his tone dripping with sarcasm.

"I...I..." stammered Ricky.

"*I is for idiot.* Is that what you think I am, Mister Sherman? An idiot?" Mr. Gleason sneered, that familiar, tired anger clouding his eyes.

Claire had been right to question his dedication; Vern Gleason had been teaching there forever, and every syllable he spoke carried the bitter weight of too many years, too many identical hallways, too many kids who just didn't care—like the one he was berating now.

"I've seen this movie before, son—and it doesn't end well. It's very simple, actually. I teach. You learn. Get a diploma. Get a job. Pay taxes. Fund my retirement. See? Simple."

Gleason turned toward the chalkboard, muttering under his breath, "Why do I even get out of bed for you people? So glad I got my Doctorate in Education."

Suddenly, a voice rang out from behind him.

"Eat….My….Shorts."

He spun around to face the class. "What? Who said that? Who said that?!"

Not a single student dared to move a muscle.

Or blink.

Or breathe.

Gleason's expression turned murderous, his already maroon complexion flushing an even redder mix of psoriasis, rosacea, and raging blood pressure.

"Well, maybe an extra chapter for tonight's review will help someone remember how to use their voice," he growled.

A collective groan echoed through the classroom.

Skype and Molly exchanged curious glances, then both looked at Andrew, sitting between them in complete silence, his eyes fixed straight ahead.

PETERSON HOUSE

Claire dropped an armful of folders onto the already cluttered front entranceway, where they landed with a loud thud among the sneakers, books, mail, and scattered papers. She kicked off her shoes with a frustrated sigh and called out to the next room, her voice heavy with exhaustion—the kind that seeped into her bones and made even the thought of moving feel like climbing a mountain.

"I hope you made yourself something to eat. Yes? No?

Well, that must be how you keep such a svelte, manly figure, huh?"

She laughed, but there was no response.

"Met a new kid today," Claire continued as she sorted through the day's mail. "Interesting case. His father is in the hospital, and they can't find his mother. He must have one. I mean, even you have a mother, *right? Right?*"

More silence.

"Sweet kid as far as I can tell. He doesn't talk much. He's the strong, silent type," she said, making her way to the next room. "And you know how I'm a sucker for the quiet ones."

Claire stood in the doorway, watching her son, ten-year-old Benjamin, sitting quietly at the table. He was deep in the zone, assembling Legos with swift, almost mechanical precision. His blonde hair, a shade lighter than Claire's, fell across his forehead as he rocked gently back and forth—a familiar self-stim that always seemed to ground him. His blue eyes, wide and clear, were fixed entirely on the interlocking plastic bricks.

There was no affect, no flicker of eye contact.

Ben existed in his own perfectly ordered world, a universe built of primary colors and precise angles.

Claire walked over and leaned down to kiss him on the forehead, but without missing a beat in his building, Ben jerked away—emotionless.

She could never get used to that.

NANA MAY PETERSON, a free-spirited aging hippie who always smelled of patchouli oil and incense, sat cross-legged on the living room floor. Her silver hair—often braided with colorful threads—fanned out around her like a halo in the flickering candlelight. She was deep in meditation, eyes closed, a faint, peaceful smile on her lips, surrounded by a perfect circle of candles. Their soft glow traced the gentle lines around her eyes and mouth.

As usual, the serenity didn't last. The trio of dogs came dashing over to greet Claire, their enthusiastic barking shattering the quiet.

"Ugh. It's like a goddamn Petco in here," Nana May snapped, struggling to command the dogs. "Sit. Sit! These dogs never listen to me."

"Aww, be nice to my babies," Claire replied, crouching down to pet her beloved trio. "Sorry I was running late this morning."

"You're always running late, my dear. You need to find balance," her earthy-crunchy mother advised.

"Can't just Zen my way through life, Ma."

"It works for me," Nana May replied, rolling up her yoga mat and blowing out the candles.

"Did Ben leave his room at all today?" Claire asked.

"Not really. You know, maybe we could try another school," Nana May suggested cautiously, aware of how touchy the subject was.

"We've been over this, Mom," Claire snapped, her irritation evident.

"I know, hon, but there are a lot of other places. I've read about one school that—" Nana May began, but Claire cut her off, her protective instincts flaring.

"Mom. I'm not... I mean, Ben's not ready," Claire corrected herself, realizing how her words had come out.

"Change is always hard," her mother said in her cheery hippie tone. "And miraculous, and terrifying, and hard again. Sometimes you just have to cross your fingers and hope for the best. Like I do."

"I'm sure if I just close my eyes and breathe through my nose, everything will be fine," Claire said, mocking her mother's advice. "Life is not all fairies frolicking on lily pads and unicorns sliding down rainbows."

"Such negative energy," Nana May sighed, shaking her head. "You used to love unicorns."

They exchanged a knowing smile, silently acknowledging their differences: Nana May, who believed her daughter needed to connect with the universe, and Claire, who thought her mother was a new-age whack-a-doodle.

Nana May cupped her daughter's face gently, and her soft hand brushed a wayward strand of hair away. Her eyes, full of concern and love, locked onto her daughter's.

"My darling little cactus tree. *'Your heart is full and hollow while you're too busy being free.'*"

"Is that from one of your meditation gurus?" Claire asked with a tone of impatience.

"Yup," her mother replied with a soft smile. "Joni Mitchell."

The back door burst open, and a whirlwind of scrambling paws and ecstatic barks erupted as Molly walked in with her backpack slung over one shoulder.

"There's my girl. Mwah!" Nana May greeted her grand-daughter with a kiss. She flashed a peace sign, grabbed her Guatemalan tote bag, and floated out the door. "Gotta run, kids. Final rose on *The Bachelor* tonight."

Molly executed a flawless, Olympic-level flop onto the couch—complete with a gold-medal-worthy eye roll so dramatic it practically left skid marks on her eyeballs, and a sigh so loud it could've powered all of Medfield. Only a teenager, truly, could wield such theatrical exhaustion.

"I can't believe how you embarrassed me at school today, Mom!"

"Please. That's part of a mother's job description," Claire replied with a silver-medal eye roll of her own. "Did you happen to see mine just float out the back door?"

"She gets to watch *The Bachelor.* Even my grandmother is cooler than I am. Are we ever gonna get a TV in this house?" Molly whined.

"You know the reason."

"I know. But it's embarrassing."

Claire cupped her daughter's face in her hand, just as her own mother had done moments earlier, and began to recite: *"I invite you to sit down in front of your television. I can assure you that you will observe…"*

"…a vast wasteland," Molly finished the sentence, pulling her chin away. "I know, Mom. You use that quote all the time. Gawd, is there anyone with an original thought anymore? I just want to know that someone understands. I need to know these people exist."

"I'm sure they do, sweetie," Claire reassured her, a quiet warmth spreading through her chest. It wasn't just the words —it was the simple fact that Molly was here.

Given everything they'd been through—her father leaving, uprooting their entire lives to move back near Nana May, and figuring out how to navigate life with her brother, Ben—the fact that Molly was even functional, that she could walk through the door with a backpack slung over her shoulder into a house that often felt like a disaster zone, filled Claire with a fierce, almost overwhelming pride.

"So, how did Andrew make out today?"

"Who?"

"The new kid in Mr. Gleason's class."

"He seems kinda bizarre," Molly said.

"Well, I think he needs a friend. You should invite him over."

"And do what?" snapped the ever-emotional teenager. "Ooh, I know. Maybe we could watch the fish tank and pretend we're exploring an underwater sea adventure. Or maybe we could paint the basement and then watch it dry."

"Don't be like that," Claire scolded.

Molly mockingly cupped her mother's face with her hand —just as her mother, and her mother's mother before her, had done—and began to recite:

"When television is good, nothing—not the theater, not the magazines or newspapers—nothing is better."

"Who says so?" asked Claire.

"Newton Minow. In that same speech," her smart-as-a-whip daughter schooled her.

"Well, I don't remember that part," Claire admitted, knowing Molly was right. "Now go say hello to your brother, smarty-pants."

Claire couldn't help but smile as Molly left the room. She turned toward the kitchen, then—

"Aaargh!" She stepped on a razor-sharp plastic Lego.

"And tell him to come pick these things up!"

OFFICER MULDOON'S APARTMENT

Andrew stood in a dim, cramped living room, his duffel bag of clothes biting into his shoulder. The air hung thick and sour, reeking of old pizza crusts and stale beer. The room was a disaster zone, a testament to the bachelor who lived among mismatched furniture and hurried habits.

A lumpy, floral-patterned sofa sagged beside a chipped faux-wood coffee table. Stacks of yellowing *TV Guide* magazines leaned precariously in the corners, threatening to topple at the slightest vibration.

Officer Muldoon, still in his starched uniform, managed an uneasy smile that didn't quite reach his eyes. His gaze flicked over the disarray, as though even he was surprised by the sheer volume of clutter, as he began the "tour."

"So, um, let's see. The kitchen is over there," he said, pointing to a tiny, cluttered space with a half-empty fridge and a greasy stove. "Living room here. Bathroom's to the left. Roger that. So, um, any questions so far?"

There was only silence—heavy, awkward silence. Andrew's eyes drifted around the room, taking in the worn carpet and the dim light that cast long shadows on the walls.

This was going to be tough. Really tough.

"Just temporary," Muldoon muttered under his breath, as if trying to convince himself. "It will be good, she said. Right? Right?"

Muldoon swung a door open, and the flick of a lamp cast a pale, yellowish glow into a bedroom. It was a stark contrast to the living room. The space was almost unnervingly neat, as if it had been preserved. This wasn't just any bedroom; it looked like it belonged to an old woman—or at least, it once had. The air was different too—not stale pizza and dust, but a faint scent of lavender and mothballs.

A simple wooden crucifix hung on the bare wall above a small maple dresser, the kind with tiny, delicate ceramic knobs. The bed was tightly made, the sheets pulled taut, crisp white even in the dim light. *Bet you could bounce a quarter off that thing,* Andrew thought. He'd seen that in an Army movie once.

Laid across the foot of the bed was a knitted blanket, probably handmade, its soft yarn faded with age, folded with meticulous care. Muldoon stood for a moment, his uneasy smile gone, replaced by a solemn expression as he took in the quiet scene. His eyes lingered on the crucifix, then the blanket, before he finally cleared his throat, breaking the spell.

"This is… well, this used to be my mother's room. She, um, she passed away a little while ago."

Andrew made eye contact for the first time. It was a connection, a small one—a momentary recognition of the loss of mothers.

"I usually fall asleep with the television on," Muldoon said, trying to fill the awkward silence. "My mother used to listen to Jay Leno every night. I was more of a Letterman guy. Now, I don't even know who the *Late Night* hosts are anymore." He glanced back at the TV in the living room with sadness. "I just… I like to leave the TV on, if that's OK."

Andrew nodded. In fact, it might have been the one thing that reminded him of home—before everything went sideways.

"Well, I'll, ah, I'll let you get settled in."

Moonlight spilled across the bed, a soft silver glow that made the unfamiliar room feel almost peaceful. Andrew sat on the edge, moving carefully so as not to disturb the neatly folded blanket.

He reached into his pocket and pulled out a small black remote—the one that had belonged to his dad. Smooth and cool against his palm, it carried a familiar weight that made the chaos of the past few days feel just a little less overwhelming.

Slowly, he lay back, sinking into the surprisingly firm mattress, and stared up at the ceiling fan's lazy, silent spin. Clutching the remote tight against his chest, the edges pressing into his skin, he held it as if he could draw comfort from it— never wanting to let it go.

MEDFIELD HIGH SCHOOL

Monday morning at Medfield High—his first real school— and it was nothing like the movies. Forget the boisterous hallways and the happy, smiling faces; here, kids streamed past like zombies, heads down, earbuds practically surgically attached, not a single person talking to anyone.

Everyone hated Mondays, sure, but this felt different—an almost tangible, robotic cloud of misery hanging in the air, thick enough to choke on.

It was ridiculous.

Skype's locker was next to Andrew's, and he could see the new kid already fumbling with the combination, brow furrowed in concentration, a bead of sweat forming on his temple. The locker seemed to mock him, refusing to budge— just another small indignity on an already intensely unhappy morning.

"Forget it," Skype told him. "Someone probably jammed the door. Or glued the lock." He knew the trick all too well—it had been pulled on his locker for years.

Just as he was about to step in to help, *WHACK!* Skype's head slammed against the lockers.

Yep. Ricky Sherman and his Sidekicks, right on cue.

Ricky snatched the cell phone from Skype's hand and held it high, just out of reach.

"Filming people when they're not looking again, Perv?" Ricky snarled, bitterness lacing his voice.

"What? Naw, dude, no," Skype replied breathlessly, trying his best to sound casual. "It's just videos. Snapchats. YouTube. You know, stuff like that."

"Yeah?" snapped Ricky, still holding the phone out of reach. "How come I never *see* anything?"

"I…I haven't posted them yet," Skype admitted sheepishly.

"Yeah, well, keep it that way, dickhead. Nobody wants to see your stupid loser videos," Ricky snarled as the Sidekicks laughed and high-fived each other like idiot cartoon characters.

"And what happened to my homework the other day?"

Taking Molly's advice, Skype responded, "My man, you really need to think for yourself. You know, form your own opinions and ideas. That's the only way you'll ever create original thought."

SLAM! His head met the locker again.

"My man?!" growled Ricky. "You better hand that homework in to Gleason. Like, today!"

"Yeah, yeah, sure," Skype replied, rubbing the side of his throbbing head. "I just thought, well, Mr. Gleason pretty much knows my handwriting and…"

"That's the problem, loser. Don't think. Just get it done. You got that… Skype?!" Ricky literally spat the word.

He tossed Skype's beloved iPhone high into the air and walked away. His brand-new phone—the one his mom would absolutely kill him over if he asked for another; the last one wasn't even paid off yet—flew above his head.

Skype watched helplessly, his eyes wide with horror, as it twirled in slow motion toward the unforgiving linoleum floor.

Just before impact, a hand shot out, quick as lightning, and snatched the device from the air. Andrew rose and handed Skype his phone.

"Thanks," Skype said, trying to recover and regain some sense of cool in front of the new kid. "My boy Ricky and I—we're always foolin' around like that."

He attempted to high-five a passing student. "Yo, what up, brother man?" But the kid ignored him. Andrew turned back to his own locker, spinning the combination and still struggling to get it open.

"Name's Skype. Not sure I can squeeze another dude into my squad, but… Yo, dap it, my man."

Skype was left hanging again by another passing student. He shook it off and said, "Whatever!"—a lame comeback straight out of third-grade recess, but it was the best he could do.

"We got it all here at Medfield High, so you're gonna wanna pick the right crew, you know?" he began, escorting Andrew and pointing out all the different groups assembled in packs along the hallway. "*Freaks. Geeks. Rainbows. Jocks. Hipsters.*"

They made their way to the courtyard.

"See that cloud of smoke? Those are the *Burnouts* and the *Stoners*—plus a few *Rockers* and *Slackers* sprinkled in every now and then," Skype pointed out. "Over there by the nicer cars? That's where you'll find the *Brains*, the *Nerds*, and the *Debate Club Dorks*. You can always tell by the black instrument cases scattered around, because most of them are in band. My mother says those are the future CEOs of America. She says you're more likely to get a college scholarship playing the oboe than by playing point guard." He looked away and mumbled under his breath, "I hope she's right. Been playing the stupid oboe since fifth grade."

They walked a bit further, with Andrew taking in every

detail around him, as if trying to memorize each sight and sound and group.

"Sitting under the trees is the *Art and Theater* crowd. You can always tell those kids because one of them is usually wearing a T-shirt with something ironic or political or has some inside joke on it that only their group 'gets.'"

Skype pointed toward a gaggle of girls.

"Then there's the cheerleaders and the *Dance Squad* crew. They're super skinny and super enthusiastic about, like, everything, and always, *always* wear the latest fashion— usually copying whatever dumb pop star is on TV that week."

Across the sprawling parking lot, in the furthest reaches from the main entrance, two figures reigned supreme: Ricky Sherman, flanked by his usual crew of brawny *Sidekicks*, held court at a couple of battered picnic tables, while the impeccably dressed and perpetually gossiping *Plastics* occupied another.

"And finally, we got the heads of the high school food chain. It can change a bit from school to school, but here it's mostly the *Plastics* and the *Jocks*. These are the kids with rich parents who give them way too much money, too much power, and a massive sense of entitlement. There are a few other pretty girls with them, but they're mostly just accessory wannabes."

Andrew was taking it all in, his eyes scanning the courtyard. He slowly began to recite, *"The brain. The athlete. The basket case. The princess. The criminal."*

Skype scrunched his face, puzzled. *"The Breakfast Club,* right?"

"Bing!" Andrew replied.

"I thought so. And, *'Eat. My. Shorts,'"* he laughed. "That was pretty ballsy."

Andrew just smirked and walked away.

Skype grinned to himself and muttered, "Ooh, I think I'm gonna like this new kid."

PETERSON HOUSE

Claire balanced on one leg, hopping slightly as she wrestled with a stubborn shoe that, despite her frantic tugs, refused to cooperate. Her messy auburn hair, slipping free of her ponytail, kept flopping into her eyes, and she blew it away with an annoyed puff. She was late—again, as usual.

"Come on, Ben!" she yelled, her voice a strained mix of desperation and impatience as it echoed into the other room. "I'm really late! Just tell me what you need, and I'll help you find it!"

She punctuated her plea with a final, forceful yank on the shoe, nearly toppling over as it finally gave way.

Then the negotiations began.

"I'll get you two toys if we can just leave now. Benjamin! We need to get to Nana May's!"

Breakfast was always a disaster. Claire closed her eyes and took deep breaths, trying to channel Nana May's calming advice. But the smell of burnt toast from the oven was impossible to ignore, a glaring reminder of how out of control her mornings had become. She tried to calm herself, but Ben's cries and frantic search for his missing dinosaur only added to the stress. She sighed, realizing that this wild, messy morning was just part of the Peterson family routine.

At this point, Ben was in full meltdown mode, his shouts and stomps growing louder as he continued his dinosaur hunt.

"Just tell me what you want! Let me help you, Ben. Talk to me!" Claire pleaded, her voice cracking under the pressure.

They were both a wreck, and it was only eight o'clock in the morning.

Living with Ben, with his autism, felt like trying to solve a puzzle where the pieces kept changing shape and the rules kept shifting. For Claire, it was a constant rollercoaster—struggling to truly connect with him, even when she felt like she was drowning in frustration.

Ben thrived on routine. His days were mapped out with

military precision—from breakfast to bedtime, every moment planned. Mornings began with the same ritual: the same cereal in the same bowl at the same time every day.

A plastic baggie of Legos sat neatly to the right, while his dinosaurs were lined up to the left. Tyrannosaurus Rex. Triceratops. Velociraptor. Brontosaurus. In that order. Always in that order.

Deviate from this, and the entire day could spiral into chaos. For the Peterson family, sticking to this routine wasn't a preference—it was essential for maintaining calm and predictability.

If only Ben could give Claire a sign, some way to communicate his needs. Talking to him was a challenge; he often shut down, leaving the family to decipher his unspoken thoughts. They relied on visual aids, hand signals, and a lot of patience to bridge the gap. It felt like playing an endless game of charades, with every conversation a new round of guessing and interpreting.

Ben's senses were always on high alert. The flicker of fluorescent lights in the kitchen, the hum of the dishwasher, or the scratchiness of certain fabrics could be overwhelming. To help him cope, the family had created a cozy corner in the living room—a haven with soft lighting, noise-canceling headphones, and calming textures. It was their way of dialing down the intensity of the outside world.

The Petersons rode an emotional rollercoaster daily. Molly learned to navigate her own feelings while offering him support. Claire, the overworked and overwhelmed single mother, did her best to keep the family unit strong.

Despite all the upheaval in their lives, Claire remained determined to find a breakthrough in communication. Maybe a shared smile or seeing Ben's face light up over something he loved would offer a glimpse of hope. It was that hope—because there is always hope—that reminded her to keep moving forward, no matter how tough things got.

MEDFIELD HIGH SCHOOL

The morning bell blared, and then it was a full-on stampede. Kids poured into the classroom, a tangled mess of arms, legs, backpacks, and bright hoodies. The noise rose instantly: some broke off into their usual little crews, still buzzing from weekend drama, while the more serious types zipped straight to their desks, already pulling out notebooks and pens.

"Please take your seats. Sit down, please," rasped Miss Ludwig, the biology teacher, her voice worn raw from years of battling teenage chatter and explaining complex biological processes. You could almost hear the friction in her vocal cords, a testament to the sheer effort it took to be heard above the noise.

Two by two, the students scrambled to sit at the lab tables. Andrew searched for an open chair, but none seemed available. Spotting an opening, he turned—and accidentally bumped into Molly. Heat rushed to his face as he quickly moved aside, desperate to avoid brushing against her again.

He shifted left. So did Molly. He shifted right. So did she, as if pulled by some invisible gravity. Their eyes locked for a moment. Awkward, fleeting—yet charged with an unusual spark. Andrew's heart pounded as he noticed the faint pink blush on Molly's cheeks.

They brushed off the moment and hurried to grab seats at the nearest table.

Skype was watching the whole exchange from his seat and immediately spotted an opportunity.

"Ah, I'm sorry, Miss Ludwig, but I refuse to take part in this barbaric ritual." He stood and declared as if he were defending some sort of king. "Frog populations are dwindling, and I couldn't live with myself if I were part of their extinction."

"Sit down, please, Michael," Miss Ludwig replied calmly, accustomed to his dramatic antics.

But Skype was already gathering his things and heading toward the door, leaving Molly alone at their assigned table.

"Besides, I'm a strict vegetarian, and, um, it's against my religion to eat meat. Or carve meat," he declared, surprising himself with his words. "I'm sorry, but I can't do it. Either way, I'm outta here."

He leaned to Andrew on his way out and whispered, *"Hasta la vista, baby.* That's from a movie."

Yeah.

Andrew knows.

Ricky Sherman shot his hand up from the back of the lab and declared, "Yo, dude. I'll partner up with Molly."

All Molly could do was sit there and roll her eyes. Could this get any worse? She had zero patience for most of the kids in her grade, especially the trio of cookie-cutter *Plastics,* but her absolute disdain was reserved for the *I'm-So-Cool-Look-at-Me Jocks* like Ricky, a guy who overused words like *awesome* and *dude* and tried to impose rules that her fiercely independent spirit refused to obey.

In a school with nearly a thousand kids, you'd think there'd be a thousand different styles. Right? But no. Instead, ten percent of the students decided how the other ninety percent should dress and act. It was easy to copy someone else's haircut or wear the same clothes. It took real guts to stand out and be yourself. Molly longed for just one person, any person, to bond with who shared those feelings—someone beyond the *Plastics* and the *Jocks.* Someone smart, funny, independent, and original. Was that too much to ask?

Miss Ludwig looked at Andrew, who was still struggling to find a table.

"Andrew, why don't you come up here and take Michael's seat?"

The chair squealed against the floor as Andrew pulled it out and sat in awkward silence beside Molly. Neither made eye contact. It was embarrassing enough when they almost headbutted each other scrambling to get into the lab, and now they had to sit together?

After what seemed like an eternity, Molly spoke.

"So, have you done this before?"

Andrew didn't answer. Molly could see he was racing around inside his head, like someone frantically opening doors and looking through cupboards, searching for the right thing to say.

"Ah, sure," he sort of shrug-nodded. "But, it…it was with penguins."

"You dissected a penguin?!" Molly exclaimed, her voice ringing out loudly. The unexpected volume drew a chorus of laughter from the class, and she immediately winced, realizing her mistake. She didn't mean to embarrass Andrew.

"I mean, I studied biology before. Sort of," Andrew replied softly, not looking up because he just wanted to slide under the desk and crawl away.

The smell of formaldehyde filled the room as Miss Ludwig opened jars and began to hand out frogs to the class. A huge frog was dropped onto the tray in front of Molly and Andrew. This thing was enormous! The arms and legs literally flowed out over the sides. Molly looked a bit squeamish.

Trying to help, Andrew turned to her and said, *"You're gonna need a bigger boat."*

Molly looked at him, confused. "Huh?"

Andrew corrected himself quickly. "Knife. I meant… you're…you're gonna need a bigger knife."

Molly gave a faint smile, thinking to herself, *He's kinda funny…and cute, in a he-doesn't-really-talk-much kind of way.*

Andrew felt a genuine surge of relief—a little more confident now that he'd actually gotten Molly to crack a smile with that *Jaws* line. It was a small win, but it felt huge. He straightened up a bit, and a faint, almost secret smile played on his own lips.

Meanwhile, Ricky Sherman sat in the back of the room,

fists clenched tightly under the desk, his eyes shooting daggers at Andrew.

CHILD PROTECTIVE SERVICES

"Excuse me, ma'am. I'm…I'm not interrupting, am I?" Officer Muldoon's voice—surprisingly gentle for someone in uniform—cut through the buzzing silence of the office.

Claire nearly jumped out of her skin. He poked his head tentatively into the doorway, his broad shoulders nearly filling the frame.

At her desk, buried under a landslide of papers, half-eaten granola bars, and what looked suspiciously like a petrified coffee cup, Claire pushed a stray strand of hair from her eyes. She must have looked like she'd just wrestled a badger—completely frazzled, with dark circles under her eyes that rivaled a raccoon's.

"Tough morning," she sighed. "I had to find a missing dinosaur."

Muldoon gave her a confused look.

"My son," she told him. "He was looking for his lost plastic dinosaur. Is there a code for that? Like a 10-56 or something?"

"10-56 is an intoxicated pedestrian, ma'am," Muldoon replied in his typical cop-speak, clearly missing the joke at first. After a beat, he realized she was kidding. "Now, if the dinosaur had been drinking, that could potentially be considered a 10-56, and well, we'd have to respond."

Claire gave a faint smile, thinking to herself, *He's kinda funny…and cute, in a he-doesn't-really-talk-much kind of way. Get a grip, Claire. What am I, fifteen?*

"Is that coffee?" she asked, looking at the cardboard tray in his hand.

"Yes, ma'am. I didn't have the intel on how you take your caffeinated beverage, so I got everything."

He wasn't kidding. The cardboard tray in his hand was

overflowing with sugars, Sweet'n Low, half-and-half, skim milk, almond milk, and flavored creams—literally everything the diner offered that could go into a "caffeinated beverage."

"Sit," Claire said, raising a hand. He obediently sat down like one of her dogs. "Well, at least someone listened to me today. Master's in Psychology, and I can't get a ten-year-old out the door in the morning."

Claire took a sip and savored her coffee as if it were the best thing she had ever tasted in her entire life. She leaned back and reflected, like she was a million miles away. "I hated being late. Even by a minute. I used to be so organized."

"I remember," Muldoon replied, letting his guard down. "You always had those colored pens and unicorn notebooks."

"God, I did love unicorns," Claire mused. "Wait, what?"

Muldoon blushed bright red. He was so busted.

"You went to Medfield High?"

"I...I was pretty quiet back then," Muldoon admitted.

"I'm so sorry, Danny. I didn't remember," Claire said, smiling with a touch of melancholy. "God, that seems like a lifetime ago. *Go Red Raiders*, right? So, how's Andrew doing?"

"Good," Muldoon replied. "I mean, I guess. I don't know. He doesn't really talk much."

Claire nodded knowingly, understanding the challenge.

"That's the reason I'm here, ma'am," Muldoon continued. "I wanted to talk to you about the living quarters situation. You see, I..."

But Claire wasn't listening—she was lost in her coffee, thinking about high school when life felt more organized. She remembered her unicorn notebooks and colored pens and days when her biggest worry was choosing the right stickers for her planner. She stared into her coffee, the steam swirling like memories.

Maybe her mother, Nana May, was right. Maybe the world needed fairies and rainbows and unicorns and quiet time and meditation. Maybe.

With a quick shake of her head, she snapped out of her trance and tried to refocus on the chaos around her.

"Any news on his mother?"

"No. No updates to report, ma'am. We've made inquiries, but as of 0900…"

Claire cut him off. "Do you always talk like that?"

"Ma'am?"

"Like you're quoting from some police manual."

"No, ma'am. Yes, ma'am," Muldoon replied, feeling embarrassed.

"Claire. It's just Claire. OK? And Danny?" she asked.

"Yes, ma'…I mean, yes, Claire."

"Next time—just a splash of almond milk. No sugar. *This is good, right? Right?*" Claire asked, trying to lighten the mood.

Muldoon smiled back. "Yep, this is good."

HIGH SCHOOL CAFETERIA, ANYWHERE U.S.A

The top three most common fears in the United States are:

1. Arachnophobia—the fear of spiders.
2. Ophidiophobia—the fear of snakes.
3. Acrophobia—the fear of heights.

So far, no one has come up with a word for perhaps the most terrifying thing on Earth—finding a seat in your high school cafeteria…as a freshman…and a new kid.

Medfield High has a student body of about 750 students, meaning roughly half the school population will be crowded into the cafeteria at any given lunch period. That's over 325 pairs of eyes fixated on your every move. Forget *Nightmare on Elm Street*, or *The Ring*, or any of the *Final Destination* movies—nothing is more terrifying or tests a kid's courage like finding a seat in the cafeteria.

Lunch at school isn't just about eating—it's a high-stakes social game that decides where you stand in the school's pecking order. Where you sit sends a clear message about who you are and who you want to be. Pick the wrong group, and you could end up with a label you can't shake. Aim too high, and rejection could be brutal. Navigating the cafeteria's unspoken rules is like walking a tightrope between fitting in and being invisible.

At Medfield High, the tables were meticulously arranged by popularity. The *Plastics* strategically positioned themselves near the bathrooms so they could access the mirrors for any last-minute beauty touch-up.

The *Jocks* claimed tables close to the food line, ensuring easy access to second and third helpings of sloppy Joes, doughy pizza slices, and fried chicken sandwiches.

The *Freaks,* with their black attire and goth make-up, gathered by the doors to the parking lot so they could head outside, smoke a cig, and maintain an air of mystery.

The *Geeks* and *Nerds* huddled in the back corner, right by the electrical outlets, ensuring their video games and laptops were fully juiced without ever worrying about a device dying.

The bell rang, and students flooded in, chatting loudly and bumping into each other as they hurried to their usual tables. It seemed like everybody knew where to sit—except Andrew.

He tried to grab a chair at the end of one long table, but a kid with way too much hair gel quickly came up behind him and said, "Sorry, dude. Somebody else is sitting there."

Andrew slowly made his way to the empty table in the farthest corner of the cafeteria. It was way, way back—where the chairs were mismatched and the Formica tabletop was covered in doodles and scratched initials.

He noticed Skype's backpack and jacket at a nearby table, tucked into the section usually reserved for loners. Sliding into an empty chair, Andrew opened the laptop Skype had left behind. He glanced around discreetly, making sure no one saw him, then quickly typed ALLISON WILDEN into the search bar.

The screen lit up with over fourteen million matches.

Teachers, doctors, students—people of every shape, size, and background—all sharing the same name.

None of them were his mother.

SLAM!

The laptop snapped shut, narrowly missing Andrew's fingers. And there, standing over him, was Ricky Sherman.

"I see Skype leeched onto you. You two are perfect for each other," Ricky remarked, his tone tinged with sarcasm and anger.

Andrew glanced around nervously. Seemed like the whole cafeteria was watching. He could definitely tell that the three *Plastics* were whispering about him because their eyes kept bouncing over to him as they talked behind their hands.

Ricky leaned in closer.

"Let me lay down a few ground rules for you, kid. I go to class, but I don't really *'go to class,'*" he said, using air quotes. "You get it? *C's get degrees*, brother. I just need to pass to keep playing on Friday nights. See, I've got a system here. A pecking order, if you will."

He gestured toward the nearby group of *Geeks* and *Nerds*. "They do the heavy lifting for me, and I let them survive high school. Fair trade, if you ask me."

Andrew listened intently. He got it. This wasn't just a Medfield High thing—it was how every school had always operated since the first bell of the very first school. The popular kids set the unspoken rules, and everyone else had to follow them. Rules about who you could sit with, who you could talk to, and where you fit in the social hierarchy.

The unpopular kids didn't make these rules, and they definitely didn't agree with them, but they had no choice but to go along and follow them. It wasn't fair—it never was. But that's just how it was.

Ricky's eyes turned to Molly, who sat alone at a table, completely engrossed in a book.

"And Molly Peterson over there? She's the smartest nerd

of all. I need her help in biology lab—so back off. Any questions?"

Since Andrew hadn't been inside the walls of Medfield High—or any high school, for that matter—Ricky's *Pecking-Order-Popular-Kid-Made-Rules* didn't apply to him. Andrew looked Ricky straight in the eye.

"Yeah, I've got a question," he replied with a hint of defiance. *"Does Barry Manilow know you raided his wardrobe?"*

A Geeky Nerd, whose thick bangs hung over his eyes like he was trying to hide behind a curtain, giggled with shocked delight.

"What? Who?" Ricky said, grabbing Andrew by the collar. "You a wise ass, kid?"

Andrew grabbed an open bag of Cheetos beside Skype's laptop and held one close to Ricky's face. "See this?" he said menacingly. *"This is this. This ain't something else. This is this."*

"What? What the…? What the hell is he talking about?" Ricky demanded, turning to the long-banged *Geeky Nerd* for an explanation. The kid just shrugged.

"You're such a freak, you know that?" Ricky said, his tone a mix of disbelief and mild unease. He shoved Andrew and hurried off, looking confused and a little spooked.

The *Nerds* and *Geeks* at their nearby table glanced over and gave Andrew a big, confident thumbs-up. He grinned to himself, feeling more comfortable with his movie quotes, thinking, *Maybe this won't be so bad after all.*

Andrew settled into the seat, trying to look casual, though his eyes kept flicking toward Molly. She was, predictably, still lost in a book—a thick paperback with a cover that looked like a cloudy galaxy. She read with deep concentration, a small, almost imperceptible smile playing on her lips, as if the characters on the page were whispering secrets only she could hear. He wished he knew what made her smile like that.

Just then, a tray clattered onto the table, rattling the cheap plastic condiments.

"Yo, Andrew," a voice drawled, as Skype dropped into the seat beside him with a thud that shook the whole table.

"Molly Peterson?" Skype said, breaking Andrew's trance. "Honestly, dude, forget it. Unless you've read, like, a million books. I heard she *reads for pleasure.* Can you believe that? Who wants to read something that's not assigned? Besides, all those books become movies anyway, and then you can just download them."

Skype jabbed his plastic fork into a mound of mac and cheese, shoveling it into his mouth. "You like movies, kid?"

Andrew raised his head, looked at Skype with a wry smile, and said, *"Dude, you have no idea."*

Chapter 2

THE JOHNSON HOUSE

Nestled on a tranquil, tree-lined street, the Johnson Dutch Colonial house stood as a beacon of tidiness. Outside, the lawn was immaculately manicured, and the shrubs were neatly trimmed. Inside, everything was meticulously arranged —clothes neatly folded in drawers, dishes cleaned and put away, the aroma of a home-cooked chicken dinner wafting from the kitchen.

"Mom, you called my phone like six times today," Skype bellowed as he burst through the back door, just off the kitchen.

"Oh, stop it. A mother can call her son any time she wants," Mrs. Johnson replied playfully, then planted a big kiss on his cheek. Andrew, who was standing awkwardly beside them, suddenly felt like an intruder.

Andrew shifted his weight, a polite smile fixed on his face. Mrs. Johnson, thankfully, recovered quickly, her gaze softening as she turned back to him.

"And who is this handsome young man?"

"This is my friend Andrew, Mom," Skype said, his voice beaming.

"Well. Very nice to meet you, Andrew. Michael never has…" She hesitated, catching herself, a small, knowing smile tugging at her lips. "I mean, he's usually not with…"

"I told you, my crew calls me Skype, Mom," her son interrupted, a slight edge of mock exasperation in his tone.

Andrew couldn't help but notice the subtle flush on Skype's cheeks—a telltale sign this was, indeed, a significant, perhaps even unprecedented, moment for him. From Mrs. Johnson's brief pause and the way her eyes lingered on Andrew, it was clear: this was the first time Skype had ever brought a friend home.

"Right…Skype," Mrs. Johnson said with a wink in Andrew's direction, effortlessly likable. She extended a hand to Andrew, her grip surprisingly firm and warm.

"Got it. Well, would your 'crew' like something to eat?"

Andrew narrowed his eyes slightly and said, *"You got any white bread?"*

"Oh, um, yes. I think we do," Mrs. Johnson replied, a bit perplexed by the request.

"I'll have some toasted white bread, please, ma'am," Andrew added.

Mrs. Johnson looked genuinely lost for a moment, trying to make sense of Andrew's request.

"He's just kidding, Mom," Skype interjected with a nervous laugh. "That's from a movie. Can Andrew stay for dinner?"

Mrs. Johnson glanced at Andrew, then back at her son, a soft smile gracing her lips. "Of course, sweetheart—if it's okay with his mother."

There was an awkward silence. Andrew, feeling the weight of the moment, knew this was a crucial juncture. Skype clearly hadn't considered that particular logistical hurdle.

Then, after a beat—"I'm sure it would be okay with her," Andrew said, his voice a little more confident than he felt.

The tension eased immediately, and Skype gave a genuine, heartfelt, "Thank you."

Skype's face immediately flushed with a mix of relief and something close to pure triumph. It was like he'd just dodged a bullet and won the lottery all at once. He grabbed Andrew by the arm and led him upstairs.

"Um, yeah, so…we're gonna go do some homework," he announced, turning back to his mother and adding with a mischievous grin, *"We're on a mission from God."*

"My brother's away at college, so I turned his room into my man cave," Skype announced proudly as they headed up the stairs.

The room was packed with cameras, computers, audio/video equipment, and an enormous flat-screen TV— the ultimate setup.

"Pretty cool, right? My squad and I usually hang here. My boy David's always like, *'Yo, my turn.'* Then Tommy's like, *'No, man, me first.'* And I'm like, *'Dudes, chill. Everyone gets a turn.'* It can get a little…crazy," Skype said with a forced laugh, trying way too hard to sound cool.

Andrew scanned the room. His eyes caught on the lone beanbag chair, slumped a little sadly beside a single Xbox controller on the floor. It practically screamed *solo* player.

An awkward silence hung in the air, thick enough to chew on. Both of them shuffled their feet, each clearly wondering who would crack first.

"Yeah, well, I, um…I invite them, but…people usually have other plans and stuff," Skype finally admitted softly, sadly. "I get to come home to all of this, though. Watch what I want. Nobody to bother me."

Andrew knew exactly how that felt—to be the odd one out, the solitary loner, isolated and overlooked. It was a sinking feeling, like being stuck on a deserted island while everyone else was having a blast on the mainland. With Skype, he'd suddenly found a rare connection—someone who understood that feeling all too well.

He reached for the game controller, squinted his eyes, and said, *"Shall we play a game?"*

"Do you always do that?" Skype asked.

"Do what?"

"Quote movie lines. That's from *WarGames,* right? And the *toasted white bread*—that's from *The Blues Brothers.*"

Andrew thought for a moment. "Sometimes it's just easier to be somebody else, ya know? You ever feel like you don't belong?"

Skype nodded, understanding perfectly. He had been trying to be cool, acting like nothing bothered him—not even the nickname "Skype" given to him in seventh grade. There were a million other cool names he would have chosen for himself. But it hurt. Pretending to be unfazed was his shield, but deep down, the nickname and the isolation stung more than he let on.

He looked at Andrew. "Wanna see something really cool?"

A closet door swung open. Andrew's eyes went wide as saucers. Shelves and shelves of DVD cases and VHS cassettes of movies filled the space. It felt like home—if only for a brief moment.

He turned to Skype and said, "Whoa, dude, you have a *serious* movie addiction."

"I know, right?" Skype laughed.

Andrew smiled. So did Skype. They were warm, happy smiles—the smiles of two kids who, for the very first time, had found a real friend.

CHILD PROTECTIVE SERVICES

Claire was heads down, shuffling through papers, unorganized as ever, when Jean Russell, her supervisor at the Suffolk County Department of Children and Families, appeared in her office.

Jean Russell was a veteran and had seen countless children pass through the system over her many years on the job. Her office, unlike some of the more chaotic workspaces around her, was a testament to her meticulous nature—files neatly stacked, reports precisely organized.

This order reflected Jean herself: a staunch rule-follower who believed in the integrity of the process. Yet beneath that structured exterior beat a genuinely kind heart. She felt deeply for the vulnerable children and families she served, her dedication rooted in a profound empathy that had only grown with each case.

It was this blend of compassion and adherence to protocol that made her such a respected—if sometimes formidable—presence in the department.

"We're gonna need to talk about the Wilden case file," she said to Claire. "Is it true that Andrew is staying with the local police?"

"Yes. Officer Muldoon," Claire responded, still looking through the mess on her desk. "It's only temporary."

"One of your *small town, small rules* applicants?" Jean asked, knowing Claire's tendency to bend the rules. She paused, her gaze steady on her subordinate, fully aware of Claire's habit of prioritizing expediency over strict adherence to procedure.

"There's a protocol, Claire. I need to review the details."

"I'm sure his file is here somewhere," Claire replied, frantically searching without any idea where anything was. Her supervisor was losing patience.

"Have you done a home study? Did it pass Physical Standards? Did you even perform a background check on Mr. Muldoon?"

Claire abruptly stopped her paper shuffling, her head snapping up with an expression of pure, manufactured surprise. Honestly, she could have won an Oscar for her portrayal of *Girl He Knew in School.*

"We went to high school together, Jean," she asserted, a touch of firmness in her voice, carefully concealing the fact that she barely recalled anyone named Danny Muldoon from her class.

Jean held her gaze, letting a silent moment pass. She knew Claire was skilled at her job and that, despite her occasional shortcuts, she always aimed to help the children in their care.

"A house just opened up. All the proper application forms have been filled out."

"But Andrew is already enrolled in Medfield. His father is—"

Jean didn't let her finish. "I spoke with the hospital, Claire. Mr. Wilden is showing severe symptoms of paranoia and delusion. He'll need individual and cognitive-behavioral therapy to ensure he's not a risk to himself or others. It could take months for his condition to stabilize."

Claire absorbed that information.

"I'm sorry, but Andrew needs to be placed in proper, certified care—at least until he's eighteen," Jean said firmly. "I'll give you a couple of weeks, but if there's nothing available locally…it's *protocol*, Claire. You should know better."

Claire watched her supervisor leave, then—with a sigh that was more groan than breath—dove back into her frantic search for the missing case file.

MEDFIELD HIGH SCHOOL

Kids hurried through the crowded halls, lost in their own worlds with earbuds firmly in place, the chatter and noise blending into a constant hum.

Andrew spent another morning wrestling with his vandalized locker. The door was jammed. Again. He gritted his teeth and pulled at the handle with all his strength, the metal biting into his palm. This was ridiculous. Frustration etched on his face, he yanked harder, desperate to get it open.

Nearby, Skype unpacked his brown-bagged lunch, carefully inspecting its contents.

"Carrot sticks and a baloney sandwich?" he exclaimed in

mock horror. "Seriously? Is she trying to punish me? At least there's spearmint gum in there. You never know when you might need minty fresh breath to save the day. Right, ladies?" he said to the trio of Plastics who breezed past him without a glance.

Skype turned and leaned against the locker. There they went, sauntering down the hallway like queens, expecting everyone else to curtsy.

"The popular kids aren't actually better than the rest of us; they just act like they are. The crazy thing is, we're the ones who give them their power. If we all stopped believing they ruled the school, they'd be nobodies. They'd have to turn on each other."

He let out a heavy, sad sigh. "Everything is just easier for them. Just once I'd like to be invited to one of their parties. I'd like to be invited anywhere."

Andrew paid them no attention. Instead, his eyes locked on a small yellow sticky note attached to the side of Skype's lunch.

"What's that?"

Skype flushed slightly. "My mom leaves me a note every day."

Andrew couldn't help but feel a pang of longing for a mother who'd leave him notes, along with carrot sticks and baloney sandwiches and spearmint gum in a brown paper bag.

"Let's see what wisdom we have today," Skype read aloud, *"The question isn't who is going to let me; it's who is going to stop me."*

"Seriously? What does that even mean?"

"That's Ayn Rand," a voice cut in. Andrew and Skype both looked up to see Molly leaning against a nearby locker. Confusion clouded Skype's face.

"She's a writer," Molly explained patiently. "She wrote *The Fountainhead* and *Atlas Shrugged*."

Andrew and Skype exchanged puzzled looks. The titles meant nothing to them.

"Are they movies?" Skype smirked.

Molly didn't answer. Frankly, she had no idea.

"Here are your Shakespeare notes," Skype told her, reaching into the locker to retrieve Molly's notebook.

"You used your own ideas, right? Original thought, remember?" Molly pleaded.

But before Skype could respond, his head was SLAMMED into the lockers, and his brown lunch bag crashed to the ground. The gum, notebooks, and sandwich spilled onto the cold linoleum floor.

Skype rolled his eyes theatrically, as if to say, *Here we go again.*

"Sorry, dude," chuckled the towering jock Ricky. "Didn't see you there."

His Sidekick cronies snickered and exchanged high-fives, reveling in the moment.

"Is that my homework down there?" Ricky asked, noticing the scattered notebook.

"No, it's…it's Molly's," Skype admitted reluctantly.

"Ooh, even better," Ricky said, bending down to retrieve her notes.

Molly leaned close to Skype. "Why do you let him walk all over you?"

"Please," he whispered back. "I have a reputation. I'm the *King of Backing Down.* Just let him blow off steam."

Ricky lunged for the notebook, but a foot slammed down on it, pinning it to the linoleum. His face burned crimson as he looked up—straight into Andrew's eyes.

Without a flicker of hesitation, Ricky's hand shot out, seizing Andrew's shirt in a white-knuckled grip, his eyes blazing with anger.

"This is the kid I told you guys about," he growled to the Sidekicks. "Acts like a weirdo, talks like a weirdo, hangs out with a weirdo. He needs a lesson on who's in charge here, boys."

Andrew held his ground. Meeting Ricky's glare with

unflinching confidence, he narrowed his eyes and said, *"Just you and me. Two hits. Me hitting you, you hitting the floor."*

Ricky hesitated, caught off guard by the new kid's boldness. He couldn't afford to back down now, not with his Sidekicks watching. He leaned in, their faces inches apart, the air crackling between them.

The tension in the crowded hallway was thick, the surrounding chatter fading as if everyone sensed this was about to become a full-blown spectacle. This could go either way.

Andrew didn't flinch. His eyes locked with Ricky's, bracing for the inevitable.

"Is there a problem here, gentlemen?" Mr. Gleason stood with his arms crossed, his stern look sharp enough to cut glass.

"Not yet," Ricky sneered through clenched teeth, finally releasing Andrew's shirt. He glanced down at the spilled lunch on the floor and barked at the Sidekicks, *"Leave the gum, take the baloney."*

Skype and Andrew exchanged a deadpan look. Seriously? No one else got that reference from *The Godfather?* The hallway was full of students who seemed oblivious, but to them, it was a moment of shared humor that went completely unappreciated.

Molly bent down to pick up her notebook. Andrew bent down closer to help, their hands briefly touching as a spark of connection passed between them. Andrew spoke softly, *"Arise, fair sun, and kill the envious moon, who is already sick and pale with grief."*

Molly looked up, surprised but pleased, recognizing the Shakespearean quote. Their eyes met, and for a moment, the bustling hallway faded into the background. Molly blushed, captivated by his words, and then quickly gathered her things and hurried away. She turned back a few times as she walked away; each time, she couldn't stop smiling to herself. It was a soft, radiant smile that stayed with her for days.

Skype turned to his friend. "So you're quoting Shakespeare now?"

"Really?" Andrew replied. "I thought that was from Leonardo DiCaprio."

POLICE STATION

Muldoon punched numbers into the phone on his cluttered desk. The police department office buzzed with activity, a mess of scattered paperwork. Harsh fluorescent lights flickered overhead, illuminating stacks of files and half-empty coffee cups that littered every surface. The air was thick with conversation, ringing phones, and the occasional burst of radio chatter.

After several rings, a familiar voice recording on the other end confirmed his frustration. He sighed, hung up, and jotted another *no answer* into a manila folder labeled: ALLISON WILDEN.

Kobolowski was at the coffee machine, pouring his fourth cup of the morning. The man practically lived on caffeine and sheer willpower to avoid sleep.

"Hey, can you still snag tickets to the Sox games?" Muldoon called out. "I'm thinking of taking Andrew. Pretty sure he's never been to Fenway."

"I doubt it. He's not exactly well-traveled," Kobolowski replied, handing Muldoon a coffee and settling in beside his desk. "The kid's never been anywhere, actually."

After a moment, he began to explain. "The old man was one of those brainiacs on Wall Street. A 'Quant.' Sort of a math whiz or statistics genius or something. He worked at Morgan Stanley for years." Stirring his coffee thoughtfully, Kobolowski glanced up and looked at Muldoon with concern. "His office was across from the World Trade Center."

Silence hung between them as Muldoon leaned in, eager to learn more about James Wilden's past.

"After 9/11, Wilden packed up and left the city. Can't

blame him, right? He moved the family to Medfield and opened up that video store. I talked to some of his old customers. They said he got stranger after Sandy Hook and the Marathon bombing—kept his wife and kid holed up, only letting them out for quick trips to the store. Said the streets are too *'nefarious.'*"

"Nefarious? Medfield?" Muldoon raised an eyebrow, almost laughing.

"I know, right? I had to look up what that word meant," Kobolowski chuckled, leaning back in his desk chair and placing a hand on his paunchy belly. "And now you're roped into watching his kid. You are hopeless, Muldoon."

"It's just temporary. She's very convincing," Muldoon admitted quietly. "Always was."

Kobolowski sat up, his eyes wide. "Was? Wait, you know her?"

"We went to high school together," Muldoon confessed. "Though she doesn't remember me."

"Who could forget a smooth talker like you?" Kobolowski teased, narrowing his eyes. "Oh, Danny Boy. You've got it bad."

"No, I don't," Muldoon denied too quickly. "Well, maybe. I don't know."

"You'll never get anywhere with women if you let them walk all over you," Kobolowski advised. "You gotta learn to play it cool. Take me and Angela. We haven't had a real conversation since the 1980s. Silent treatment. It's the secret to a happy marriage. *'Ooh, my feelings. My emotional journey. You don't communicate.'* In my house, I'm the boss. I wear the pants."

Muldoon rolled his eyes at Kobolowski's macho act. Just then, Officer Caroline Butler strolled by, grabbing a coffee from the communal pot. Her calm demeanor and easy smile were a stark contrast to Kobolowski's testosterone.

"Hey, guys," she greeted them casually.

Muldoon instantly fumbled. He straightened up and immediately shifted into his professional cop mode. "Good morning, Officer Butler. We were, um, just retrieving our caffeinated beverages."

Caroline smirked, teasing him gently. "Good for you. I'm just 'retrieving a caffeinated beverage' myself."

Kobolowski looked at his partner and shook his head. "Hopeless."

He was right. Danny Muldoon had absolutely zero game with women.

MEDFIELD HIGH SCHOOL

Andrew and Skype walked through the courtyard toward the parking lot, navigating the diverse cliques that defined the school's social landscape.

They passed through a haze of cigarette and vape smoke from the *Burnouts* and *Stoners,* doing their best not to make eye contact. They stepped over a pile of black instrument cases marking the territory of the *Brains, Dorks,* and *Nerds,* all of whom were engrossed in conversations about science projects and math problems.

On a small patch of lawn, the *Art and Theater* crowd passionately rehearsed a song from the school's production of *Wicked.* Their energy was infectious, even if Andrew didn't know the lyrics.

In the end zone of the adjacent football field, the *Cheerleaders* and *Dance Squad* perfected a tricky pyramid routine, their synchronized movements a testament to hours of dedication and practice.

The *Goths,* decked head-to-toe in black, watched everyone with a mix of curiosity and indifference. Andrew and Skype exchanged a glance, silently bonding over the shared feeling of not fitting in with the mainstream crowd.

Finally, they passed gleaming new Range Rovers and oversized Suburbans—cars perfectly tailored to the egos of the *Plastics* and spacious enough for the rich *Jocks'* sports gear. These stood in stark contrast to the tired Chevy Novas and leased Honda Civics that belonged to their public school teachers.

"So, have you talked to Molly yet?" Skype asked Andrew as they strolled through the parking lot. "You know, as 'Normal Guy Andrew,' not 'Movie Guy Andrew'?"

"Trust me," Andrew replied. "*Movie Guy Andrew* is way cooler. And a lot more interesting."

"Of course, that Andrew is more interesting," Skype agreed. "She's never seen any of those movies."

"Wait, seriously?"

"Yep," he confirmed. "I heard she doesn't even have a television. Can you believe that? In this day and age? That's child abuse, man!"

As they talked, they looked up to see Molly jogging toward them, arms full of books clutched to her chest, her ponytail swinging with each stride.

"Hey, guys," she greeted, a bit breathless. "Andrew. Hi. Um, my mom was wondering… she thought it might be a good idea… do you want to come over? I have all my biology notes at home, and, well, since we're lab partners and everything…"

Andrew fought to keep the excitement from his face, a sudden surge he definitely didn't want anyone to see.

Beside him, Skype froze mid-stride. "Wait. What about all that *'original thought and think for yourself'* stuff?" he interjected.

Molly shrugged innocently, then turned to Andrew. "So, four o'clock?"

Andrew smirked, squinted his eyes playfully, and replied, *"I was just about to say—four o'clock."*

As Molly floated away on air, Skype gave Andrew a playful punch on the arm.

"Dude, she's totally smitten. Like, *'You're her density.'*"

"You do realize the girl in *Back to the Future* was his mother, right?" Andrew pointed out.

"I know," Skype chuckled. "Pretty messed up." He took a

few steps, then paused. "You gotta admit, though, she was kinda hot, right?"

Andrew playfully punched him on the arm—and judging by Skype's exaggerated overreaction, it was clear he wasn't expecting the hit to be so strong.

PETERSON HOUSE

Andrew wandered through the Peterson living room, his fingers skimming slowly over each book stacked high on the floor and filling the shelves. History. Poetry. Autobiography. Fiction—everything he could ever want to read was within reach, housed in the cluttered Victorian home in Medfield.

It reminded him of the days he used to explore his parents' video store as a child—when he would hear the laughter of children outside and rush to the window to watch them pass by. He remembered how his mother would place a comforting hand on his shoulder and whisper in his ear. He shook the memory from his head when Molly broke the silence.

"Can I get you anything to eat?"

"*You got any dry white toa...?*" Andrew started, but caught himself. "No. Um, thank you. I'm good."

His eyes scanned the room, noting something unusual. Molly, catching his gaze, knew exactly what he was thinking. Everyone seemed to have the same reaction when they visited the Peterson house.

"Yeah, um, we don't have a television. Pretty lame, right?" she admitted with a shrug. "We do a lot of reading here."

"No, I think that's really cool," Andrew replied, and he genuinely meant it. The absence of a TV felt almost refreshingly genuine—like a throwback to simpler, quieter times.

"Thanks," Molly said warmly, her admiration for him growing.

Andrew's attention snagged on the adjacent playroom, where Ben sat in a world of his own, completely absorbed in his Legos and a small herd of toy dinosaurs. Molly introduced him with a cheerful smile. "That's my brother. Ben, this is Andrew."

But Ben didn't respond; his focus was solely on arranging his toys with meticulous care. Molly noticed Andrew's curiosity and leaned closer, whispering, "He's kind of… well, he can be a little… different."

Andrew didn't miss a beat. Meeting Molly's eyes, he quoted softly, *"We're all pretty bizarre. Some of us are just better at hiding it, that's all."*

Molly absorbed his words as if they were the most profound she had ever heard. There was something about Ben that drew Andrew in—a sense of loneliness, the feeling of being trapped in his own world. Maybe it was the gentle rocking that reminded him of his father huddled in the corner of the bedroom that morning. Or maybe Andrew simply saw a bit of himself in Ben.

He approached cautiously, but Molly intervened. "Don't. He really doesn't like it when people…"

But Andrew wasn't listening. He had already knelt down beside the young boy, who looked up at him with wide, curious eyes.

Molly's own eyes widened in wonder as, without a word, Ben suddenly held out a Lego piece to Andrew.

They sat together in a comfortable silence, two heads bent, hands clipping plastic bricks with a shared, intense focus. It was such a simple act—yet to Molly, it was nothing short of extraordinary. In all her years, she had never seen her little brother make a genuine connection with anyone before.

JOHNSON HOUSE

Skype sat alone in his makeshift Man Cave, scrolling through the internet, the room bathed in the white light from a computer screen.

Click—click—click.

He landed on his personal YouTube page, a collection of videos he'd made with his cell phone. Most featured him roaming the halls of Medfield High, shouting things like, *"Whaddup, ladies!"* and *"Yo, my man!"*—only to be met with hands pushing the camera away. Other clips showcased his witty observations about school, teachers, society, and the social hierarchy of *Plastics* and *Jocks.*

They were good. Really good. And funny. But no one had ever seen them. His subscriber count stood at eight—that included his mother, his father, his older brother, four of Mrs. Johnson's friends, and some random dude from Texas who kept messaging him to chat.

Skype's right hand hovered over the mouse, fingertips tingling with nervous energy. He toggled the cursor between the *PRIVATE* and *PUBLIC* icons, debating whether to finally share his videos.

Should he? Should he show everyone how funny and nice and witty and cool he could be? Maybe then they'd see he wasn't a *Freak,* or a *Nerd,* or a *Loser.* Maybe they'd like him. Maybe they'd invite him places.

The cursor lingered over the *PUBLIC* button…

"Forget it," he muttered softly, sadly. "Maybe tomorrow."

Click.

The screen shifted to his Facebook page. He scrolled over the *FIND FRIENDS* icon. No new friend requests. He moved to *VIEW SENT REQUESTS.* None had been accepted. The sting of rejection was palpable as he closed the laptop just as his mother entered the room.

Her maternal instincts immediately kicked in and sensed something was wrong. Mothers know. They always know.

"That boy the other day seemed nice," she said, her voice soft and laced with the quiet hope of cheering up her lonely son.

"Yeah, he's pretty cool. He's the one I told you about. His parents and everything."

"Such a shame," replied kind-hearted Mrs. Johnson.

"He's actually a really cool dude. He's pretty funny and uses movie lines that crack me up. Plus, he's really smart. I thought he'd be way behind because he was homeschooled and stuff, but in most things, he's way ahead of me. Maybe not a genius or anything, but he's definitely up there."

"Well, you tell Andrew he's welcome here anytime, okay?"

"I will, Mom. Thanks."

Mrs. Johnson leaned down and pressed a soft, loving kiss to his forehead, a secret, fervent wish forming in her mind: if only a mother's kiss could make him truly popular and confident.

MULDOON'S APARTMENT

Muldoon walked into the apartment, juggling a pizza box and grocery bags, his uniform lightly rumpled from a long day. The smell of pepperoni and cheese filled the air as he kicked the door shut behind him. Andrew sat on the couch, staring blankly at the TV screen, clutching his father's old remote in his hand like a lifeline. The low murmur of an old black-and-white movie played in the background, one Andrew had watched a hundred times.

Muldoon let out a tired sigh, setting the pizza on the cluttered coffee table and the grocery bags on the kitchen counter. He looked around, searching for some way to inject normalcy. He just needed to find a way—any way—to smooth the sharp edges of this forced, newfound relationship.

"Hey, I brought dinner," he announced, hoping to break the heavy silence.

Andrew just stared at the screen.

"Use this one," Muldoon said, tossing a more modern remote onto Andrew's lap. "It actually works."

He unpacked the groceries, trying to fill the silence. "So, how was school today?" Muldoon asked, glancing over hopefully.

Andrew didn't respond.

"Did Miss Peterson say anything about me?" he asked, trying to mask his eagerness.

Still nothing.

"I was never much of a talker either," Muldoon admitted, opening the pizza box. "I guess I'm out of touch with what teenagers talk about these days. Back in my day, it was all about girls and beer and getting in trouble. I'm a cop now, so I think we better just stick with girls, okay?"

Nada. Zip. Zilch.

Muldoon stopped what he was doing and looked over at Andrew with a stern face.

"You know, *it's legal for me to take you down to the station and sweat it out of you under the lights.*"

Andrew looked up, recognizing the line.

"I'm just kidding. That's from a movie or something," Muldoon said with a grin, finally cracking the tension. Andrew nodded knowingly. Yeah. He knows. Warren Beatty said that in *Dick Tracy.*

"I only have one question," Muldoon continued. "Sausage or pepperoni?"

"Pepperoni," Andrew replied softly.

Finally, a connection! Muldoon enthusiastically set the pizza down and opened the fridge.

"Alright, let's try another. Root beer or Coke?"

"Root beer."

"Okay, here we go!" Muldoon cheered. "I guess Kobolowski was wrong. I can communicate!"

Pleased with the small victory, Muldoon grabbed a slice and joined Andrew in the living room.

"So," he said, looking at his watch. "It's still early. You wanna watch something?"

"I could go for a movie," Andrew replied, talking through a mouthful of pizza and feeling more at ease.

Muldoon grabbed the remote and started flipping through channels, talking non-stop and thinking aloud with each click.

Click.

"I was never good at talking," he admitted.

Click.

"And girls? Forget about it."

Click.

"Especially Claire. She was so intimidating in high school. I still get tongue-tied around her."

Click.

"How do you even communicate with someone like that?"

Click.

"'Lack of communication.' What does that even mean?"

Click.

"Girls are complicated, aren't they? I have no idea what they want."

Click.

"Do you know what they want? I certainly don't."

Andrew rolled his eyes internally. *Jeez, for someone who says he doesn't talk much, this guy won't shut up!*

Finally, Muldoon stopped clicking and landed on a movie. He glanced at Andrew with a side-eye, silently asking if it was okay. Andrew responded with a casual shrug that said, *I'm good if you are.*

"You seen this?" Muldoon asked.

"I've seen *everything*," Andrew replied.

Then two Lay-Z-Boy recliners tilted back simultaneously, accompanied by the soft hiss of cans cracking open—Budweiser for Muldoon, root beer for Andrew—and the two roommates settled in to watch Ryan Gosling charm Rachel McAdams in *The Notebook*.

SHERMAN HOUSE

Everyone assumed Ricky Sherman would get a football scholarship. His brother got a full ride to play at the University of Rhode Island. His sister earned tuition reimbursement to play field hockey at Assumption. His dad had been a two-way starter for UMass and made the scout team with the Giants.

His mom received grant money for being a scholar-athlete at Stonehill.

So when Ricky started struggling with his grades in middle school, he did the only thing he could think of to get better test scores—cheat. Study harder? Focus more? Pay attention? No way. And there was no chance he'd let his parents meet with his teachers for help. Everyone knows when a parent is seen in the hallways at three o'clock, it's either because their kid is in trouble or there's an IEP meeting. God forbid your friends see them.

At least those kids' parents showed up! Ricky's parents had gone through a war-like divorce and couldn't stand to be in the same room together—it always ended in a shouting match. How his dad cheated on his mom. How his mom snuck vodka into her drinks.

"Loving" perfectly describes some parents—but what about the opposite? How do you describe parents who don't seem to care at all? Neglectful? Egotistic? Lame? In Ricky's case, it was all of the above.

The old man was distant and angry, only wanting to talk about how Ricky should play better and work out more. And his mother? Well, Mrs. Sherman wore a happy face for the rest of the world but had nothing left for her youngest son.

C's get degrees became Ricky's motto. Just do enough to keep getting by—and when that didn't work, bully someone into doing the work for you. So instead of being embarrassed by bad test scores, Ricky got angry. Then he got mean. Real mean.

Those emotions fueled him on Friday night football fields all over Norfolk County. Players from rival towns like Westwood, Hopkinton, and Millis all felt Ricky Sherman's wrath. Some kids even had the scars and broken bones to prove it.

Ricky needed to keep his grades slightly above average if he had any hope of following the Sherman family scholarship tradition. But since he'd failed to hand in Mr. Gleason's homework assignment, even pulling off a C in that class seemed like a real stretch.

Since the divorce, Ricky split his time between his dad's apartment across town and his mom's place. They had no clue what he really wanted in life—because they never asked.

The Shermans didn't know that, deep down, Ricky really hated sports. What he truly loved—what he was most passionate about—was music. He even snuck out for guitar lessons for a few months, but once his dad realized the sessions interfered with his *Select* travel team schedule, that was it. No more music. No more guitar.

See, that's the problem with *Select* teams like *Top Tier*, *A1*, *All Star*, and *Elite*: you start to believe it. You think you're better than everyone else—because the coaches have already told you that. You've been handpicked, grouped with other *Select* kids, wearing matching uniforms, practicing for hours every week. You spend so much time together, traveling to tournaments and hanging out after games, that you pretty much have to be friends.

It creates a bubble where you all start to think you're invincible.

RICKY GLANCED up and down the deserted school hallway, ensuring he was alone, before slipping into Mr. Gleason's empty classroom. His heart raced as he checked once more for any sign of a teacher or student. Satisfied, he approached the teacher's desk and carefully opened the top drawer. Inside lay a neat stack of papers, and among them was the prized possession he was looking for—the midterm exam. Ricky pulled out his cell phone and snapped a quick photo of the questions.

As he began to replace the papers, his eyes caught sight of a folder marked **ANDREW WILDEN**. Ricky couldn't resist. He opened the folder and quickly scanned the report. His expression shifted from casual mischief to wide-eyed surprise. Before he could delve deeper, the bell rang, jolting him back to reality. Panicked, he hastily returned the folder to its place just as Mr. Gleason entered the room.

"Mister Sherman?" Gleason exclaimed with a hint of surprise. "Well, nice to see you here early for once. Getting a head start on studying for the midterm?"

Ricky flashed a snarky smirk, his mind racing. "Oh, I should be all set, Mr. Gleason," he replied smoothly. "Let's just say I have a *photographic* memory."

Gleason raised an eyebrow, but before he could question further, the class began to fill up. Ricky slipped into his seat, his thoughts still reeling from what he had glimpsed in Andrew Wilden's folder.

POLICE STATION

"Need to show you something," Kobolowski grunted, heaving a large brown cardboard box marked EVIDENCE onto Muldoon's cluttered desk. "We found this hidden in the back of Allison Wilden's closet."

Muldoon stood and began to sift through the contents, his face tightening with concern.

"Has Andrew seen this?" he asked, his voice edged with worry.

"No. I thought you should see it first," Kobolowski replied, his tone serious.

Across the station, Officer Butler called out, "Your wife's on the phone."

"Tell her I'm busy," Kobolowski huffed, doing his best to maintain a tough, macho façade.

Officer Butler shot back, unimpressed: "Tell her yourself. You better hurry—she sounds upset."

Suddenly, Kobolowski's face softened, the usual tough-guy mask melting away. He picked up the phone, panic flickering in his eyes, and his voice shifted to a gentler tone as he spoke softly, lovingly.

"Hello?" he said, a bit of fear in his voice.

Angela Kobolowski was a force to be reckoned with—never one to be pushed around.

"Yes, dear," he started. "Yes, of course... I'm sorry, sweetie... No, my love... I will... I... I gotta go. Bye."

Officer Butler glanced over at Danny Muldoon and smirked. "Who wears the pants?"

But Muldoon wasn't listening—he was too absorbed in the contents of the EVIDENCE box his partner had dropped on his desk.

PETERSON HOUSE

Saturday. Finally, a day off. A day to get organized. Claire surveyed her living room: books stacked haphazardly, dog toys scattered everywhere, Ben's Legos and toy dinosaurs littering the floor like a minefield. She sighed, feeling overwhelmed. *I really need to get my life together,* she thought.

The doorbell rang. Claire glanced at the clock and felt a wave of relief wash over her—thank God. Another distraction. Another reason to put off the daunting task of organizing. She pulled her hair into a tight ponytail and walked to the door, actually grateful for the interruption.

She opened it to find Officer Danny Muldoon standing on her doorstep.

"Afternoon, ma'am... I mean, Claire," he greeted nervously. With her hair pulled back, she looked younger, softer—like the girl he remembered from high school.

Muldoon fumbled for his words, struggling to recall why he was there. "I, um, I was told Andrew was here? He's been studying with your daughter..." He glanced at his ever-present notepad. "Molly, is it?"

"Danny! Come in," Claire replied, excited to see him at the door. *Anything to not have to tidy up!* "Andrew's at the Johnsons' with Skype. But come in. Let me get you the coffee this time."

"No, thank you. I'm taking the boys to a Red Sox game," he explained.

Just then, Nana May peeked her head around the corner.

"Claire, you didn't tell me it was Daniel Muldoon at the door. You two went to high school together."

"Yeah, I know, Mom. Jeez," Claire muttered, rolling her eyes hard—trying to cover up the fact that she hadn't remembered.

Nana May stepped forward and took Muldoon's hand warmly. "I was so sorry to hear about your mother, Daniel. She was a wonderful lady. She had a kind soul."

"Thank you, ma'am," Muldoon said respectfully, though his eyes flickered to the giant marijuana leaf splashed across Nana May's *Legalize Weed* T-shirt.

"Ma'am?" Nana May looked pointedly at Claire. "Oh, so this is the man you were going on and on about. 'Ma'am' this. All 'official' that. If I didn't know better, I'd think my daughter had a schoolgirl crush on you, Daniel."

Claire was utterly embarrassed, and Daniel Muldoon turned bright red—almost purple. Nana May, however, was unfazed. With a firm grip, she took Muldoon by the elbow and ushered him inside the cluttered house.

"Come in, Daniel. I insist," she declared, her voice leaving no room for argument.

Still reeling, Daniel stumbled through the doorway, his eyes widening as he took in the teetering stacks of books, the sprawl of Legos across the coffee table, and several toy dinosaurs scattered throughout the room.

"Thank you, ma'am," Muldoon replied politely.

"Call me Nana May," the aging hippie declared, waving her arms theatrically. "It's short for Maya—my Hindu name. It means Magic."

Claire leaned toward Danny and whispered, "Her real name is Martha."

Nana May practically dragged Muldoon inside as the dogs swarmed around him, tails wagging and tongues lolling. As he stumbled further in, Muldoon spotted Ben in the corner, completely absorbed in a world of Legos and dinosaurs.

"Afternoon, son. How you doin' there?"

Ben didn't respond. Muldoon glanced at Claire and asked, "Does your son like baseball? I'd be happy to take him along."

"No, thank you," Claire replied firmly.

"I don't mind, really."

"I really don't think it's a good idea," she reiterated.

"Well, I think that's a great idea!" Nana May chimed in, full of enthusiasm.

Claire shot her mother a hard, exasperated look. Muldoon persisted, "Really, it's no problem at all."

"No, thank you. Ben has a routine," Claire replied to him firmly.

"Claire, let him go," pleaded Nana May.

"The station gets plenty of tickets," Muldoon continued, undeterred. "You could all come."

"Oh, wouldn't that be fun!" exclaimed Nana May, her eyes sparkling with excitement.

Muldoon approached Ben with a friendly smile. "Every kid likes baseball. Ben, is it? Come on, Ben, let's…"

Before he could finish his sentence, Claire reacted swiftly and sharply. "I said no. Enough! I don't want him to go!"

Muldoon froze, stunned by Claire's sudden outburst. The room fell into an awkward silence, everyone visibly shaken—especially Ben, who started to cry at the intensity of his mother's reaction. Nana May hurried to comfort him, her disappointment glaring in her eyes as she shot daggers at her daughter.

"I… I'm sorry," Muldoon stammered, confused and embarrassed. "I didn't mean to... Of course. I'm so sorry, Ben. Mrs... Nana... May... Martha... Well, I'll just... I better go get the boys."

Muldoon turned quickly, eager to leave the uncomfortable

tension hanging in the room. Claire felt guilty as she watched him hastily retreat out the door. She wanted to apologize, to explain the complexities of her life—how some days were harder than others, how she wished she could go back to the days of colored pens and unicorn notebooks—but the words wouldn't come. She simply stood there silently as Danny Muldoon climbed into his car and drove away.

JOHNSON HOUSE

Andrew sat alone in Skype's bedroom, waiting for him to return from the basement after Mrs. Johnson finally—mercifully—made him pick up the dirty laundry.

He scanned the shelves above the computer: seashells from trips to the beach, pictures from a Disney World vacation, spelling trophies from grade school—all the things Andrew had never gotten to experience. His eyes landed on a framed photo of Skype with his parents and older brother. The perfect happy family.

Turning his attention to the computer, Andrew clicked open Skype's Facebook page. With a deep breath, he moved the cursor to the search bar and typed *Allison Wilden*.

A slew of profiles appeared. A selfie of a young woman in sunglasses on a beach, her bio simply reading: *Loves dogs, coffee, and traveling!* Another profile for *Allison Wilden Photography*, its icon a camera lens and tagline: *Capturing life's beautiful moments in the Pacific Northwest*. Then there was Allison "Allie" Wilden, her profile picture a cartoon illustration, her bio reading: *Avid reader, aspiring chef, and cat lover*.

None of them were his mother.

Frustrated, he minimized Facebook, revealing a YouTube page filled with Skype's short films and clips. Andrew was just about to click on one when Skype burst into the room, slightly out of breath, clutching a basket of laundry.

"Don't touch that!" he cried, dashing across the room and

slamming his hand on the mouse to minimize the page. "You almost posted them!"

Andrew, missing the panic entirely, just stared at the screen. "Did you make these movies?" he asked. "They look pretty cool."

Skype shrugged, trying to deflect the hurt. "They would only get, like, ten views anyway."

After a moment, he confessed quietly, "Do you know I only have fourteen followers on Instagram? Most of them are my family—and a few weirdos in Texas. I send out friend requests on Facebook, but no one ever..."

He trailed off, realizing the weight of admitting this sad truth aloud for the first time.

"I see all the pictures they post. Birthday parties. Trips to the mall. Everyone hanging out at a friend's house." He hesitated, then asked, "Do you know why they call me *Skype*?"

"I figured it's because of all your computers and AV equipment," Andrew replied.

"I got sick in seventh grade. I had to spend most of the year at home. They set up a computer and put a camera in the classroom so I could see the teacher and the board and stuff. You know—*Skype*. I was stuck in my room the whole time. I could still hear the kids talking and laughing. Every now and then, someone would stick tape on the lens so I couldn't see or bump the camera so it was pointed to the floor."

He paused to collect himself, staring at the computer as if he needed support and answers, the pain of the past unearthed. "Do you have any idea what it's like to watch your whole world through a stupid little screen?"

Andrew smirked. It was slight and barely perceptible, but he knew exactly how Skype felt. They both knew the feeling of isolation and hiding behind screens. But for them, watching a movie was more than just entertainment; it was an escape into a world where anything seemed possible, a belief that everything in life was as magical as it seemed in the movies. They could go anywhere and be anyone.

"You've been watching long enough," Andrew said softly. Then, almost to himself, he whispered, "We both have."

Skype nodded and let the words sink in for a few minutes.

"Yo, Crew," Mrs. Johnson interrupted, standing in the doorway. "Officer Muldoon is downstairs. He's very… official, isn't he?" she said with a smirk. "Wear your jackets; it might get chilly at the game," said the overprotective mother. "And remember to have fun, you two."

Mrs. Johnson lovingly kissed her son on the forehead. Then she leaned down, hugged Andrew, and kissed him on the forehead too. He beamed.

"Thanks," he said softly. "Nobody's done that to me in a while."

Mrs. Johnson smiled at him warmly. "Well, you'll get plenty of those here."

FENWAY PARK

A cool spring night in Boston for a Red Sox game, the air was thick with the smell of Italian sausage, grilled onions, and stale beer. Andrew and Skype sat along the third base line, eating hot dogs, chewing pretzels, and drinking sugary soda. With every pitch, they rattled off a line from a baseball movie, cracking each other up—and bugging the living shit out of Officer Muldoon.

"'*Juuuust a bit outside,*'" yelled Skype.

"'*Pick me out a winner, Bobby,*'" replied Andrew.

"'*You're killing me, Smalls. You're killing me!*'"

"'*There's no crying in baseball!*'"

"'*Hey batta batta hey batta batta batta SWING batta!*'"

Muldoon had enough. "Oh my God, stop!" He looked at Andrew. "First, I can't get you to talk, now you won't shut up!"

The teenagers burst out laughing, having the time of their lives.

"What's with you guys and the movie lines?" Muldoon asked. "Can't you just talk like normal people, for crying out loud?"

Skype looked at Muldoon. "Can't you?"

"What's that supposed to mean?"

"Please, I've seen you around Molly's mom. You're hopeless, dude," Skype told him. "'Yes, Ma'am. No, Ma'am. That's a 10-57, Ma'am.' You're all, like, RoboCop and stuff."

Andrew laughed. "*Serve the public, protect the innocent, uphold the law.*"

Muldoon tried to brush it off. "Oh, like you guys would know how to talk to a girl."

After a moment of silent reflection, he thought better and asked—actually pleaded, "Do you guys know how to talk to a girl?"

"Trust me," said Skype, full of confidence and ripping into his third hot dog. "They love movies more than guys do. You want to impress a girl? Tell her you felt sorry for Katniss Everdeen in *The Hunger Games* but respected her strength and courage. Or admit you watched *A Walk in the Clouds* all the way through. And if you really want them to fall for you? Tell them you cried during *The Notebook.*"

Muldoon and Andrew immediately looked at each other with guilty glares, as if to say, *I didn't cry!*

Muldoon thought for a bit as he watched the pitcher slowly rub the baseball between his hands, contemplating his next pitch.

"So, you guys really think watching movies could help?" Muldoon asked sincerely, looking for guidance.

Skype and Andrew looked at each other, and their eyes suddenly widened as an idea formed—and they began to hatch a plan.

MULDOON'S APARTMENT

Andrew stood beside a tall AV cart, dressed in his father's white smock and bow tie. He looked more like a mad scientist than a teacher about to educate his student on how to date a woman. The metal shelf just below the TV was stacked with old VHS tapes—classic romantic comedies like *Say Anything*, *Annie Hall*, and *The Princess Bride* mixed in with some lesser-known titles.

He addressed the small "class" of two in front of him, holding a long wooden pointer in one hand and a black remote control in the other.

"Alright, everyone, settle in. Let's see what we have today. Ooh, Social Studies," Andrew said, mimicking his father's tone as he slid a tape from its sleeve. "*When Harry Met Sally*—Rob Reiner's touching romantic comedy that begs the question: can men be friends with women without wanting sex?"

Skype and Muldoon exchanged glances. This was going to be interesting.

Andrew inserted the tape into the VCR, and the screen flickered to life. Billy Crystal began speaking to Meg Ryan with an exaggerated silly accent.

"Waiter, there is too much pepper on my paprikash."

Meg Ryan echoed, *"Waiter, there is too much pepper on my paprikash."*

"But I would be proud to partake of your pecan pie," Crystal replied.

Muldoon sat at a tiny desk, furiously taking notes like an athlete studying game film. His brow furrowed in concentration, his pen racing across the paper as his eyes darted between the television and his notes. The "student" captured every detail, every line.

Skype leaned back in his chair, propped his feet up, and smirked. "A vast wasteland, my ass."

MEDFIELD

Andrew and Skype sat in the front seat of Mrs. Johnson's minivan, face to face, eye to eye. The air was thick with seriousness as they each took a deep breath.

"You sure about this?" Andrew asked.

"Never been surer of anything in my life," said an overly confident Skype.

"I don't know," replied a reluctant Andrew.

"Listen to me," Skype told him. "You've studied hours of DVDs. Memorized miles of VHS tapes. Play, rewind, play, rewind again—all in preparation for this very moment. My friend, you are ready." He paused, then in his best Yoda voice added, *"There is no try. Only do."*

Andrew took a deep breath, nodded, and slowly began to clap.

CLAP... CLAP... CLAP...

Skype immediately waved him off.

"No. No. We're not... we're not doing the 80's-teen-movie-slow-clap thing."

Over the next few weeks, Andrew took Molly on a series of dates, each one reenacting a famous scene from a romantic comedy:

PRETTY WOMAN – Skype gripped the minivan's steering wheel, knuckles white. His mom would absolutely murder him if she found out he was driving on just a learner's permit. He hunched low in the seat, practically invisible, darting nervous glances at every parked car and passing pedestrian.

Then he saw her—Molly, walking home from school, backpack slung over one shoulder.

Just as he was about to cruise past, Andrew's head burst through the sunroof, a huge, goofy grin plastered across his face.

"Hey, Molly!" he yelled, thrusting a single red rose in her direction.

Molly's eyes went wide, a blush creeping up her neck and

onto her cheeks. She giggled, reaching out to take the rose as Skype prayed he'd make it home without getting caught.

SAY ANYTHING – Molly hunched over her desk, wrestling with homework, when music suddenly ripped through the quiet. Peter Gabriel's *In Your Eyes* blared, loud enough to rattle the windowpanes. Curiosity tugged her to her feet and toward the open window. There was Andrew, standing on her front lawn, wearing a long, ridiculous brown trench coat and holding a boombox.

THE NOTEBOOK – Andrew and Molly sat in a rowboat in the middle of Kingsbury Pond, the water reflecting the golden hues of the setting sun. They gazed into each other's eyes as the world around them seemed to fade away.

Hidden in the bushes by the water's edge was Skype, ready to recreate the romantic lake scene—only instead of swans, he had brought little yellow rubber duckies.

One by one, the ducks floated past the rowboat. Molly burst into laughter as the numbers grew—one, ten, fifty—until they were soon surrounded by a sea of yellow.

Mission accomplished, Skype turned to leave—and bumped straight into Officer Kobolowski. He was *so* busted.

TITANIC - Andrew carefully walked Molly along the edge of King Philip Overlook, a scenic mountain trail with views of the Charles River and the surrounding woods of Medfield.

As they leaned against a safety railing, Andrew removed her blindfold to reveal a breathtaking view, the town spread out below them like a miniature world.

Molly was nervous at first, but Andrew held her close, his arms steady and reassuring. They leaned close to the edge, the wind blowing in their faces, making them feel alive and free. Andrew stood on the railing, lifted his arms, and shouted like Jack Dawson.

"I'm the king of the world!"

Molly laughed, her fear melting away.

SIXTEEN CANDLES - Molly and Andrew sat cross-legged on top of a picnic table in quiet Hinkley Park, a cake with lit candles between them. The soft glow illuminated their faces as they looked deeply into each other's eyes, just like Samantha and Jake in the movie.

Andrew's expression was gentle and sincere, his eyes reflecting the flickering candlelight. Molly felt a flutter in her chest, her heart pounding as she realized how much she liked him.

Andrew's creativity knew no bounds. Molly, who had never seen these movies, found herself swept off her feet. She began to see Andrew as the most romantic, thoughtful, funny, and original boy she had ever met.

They were falling in love.

MEDFIELD POLICE STATION

Claire stepped into the lobby of the busy police station, holding a cardboard tray of coffee. The station was a hive of activity, with officers bustling about, phones ringing, and the hum of conversation filling the air. The fluorescent lights cast a harsh glow over the room, highlighting the worn linoleum floors and scuffed walls. Claire navigated through the chaos, her eyes scanning for a familiar face as the rich aroma of freshly brewed coffee wafted from her tray.

She took a deep breath, steadying herself before heading toward the front desk, and muttered under her breath, "This is good, right? *Right?*"

"Excuse me," she spoke up. "I'm looking for Officer Muldoon."

"What's this regarding?" Officer Caroline Butler asked, eyeing her up and down.

"It's a Child Protective Services matter," Claire said, lowering her voice. "I really would like to speak with him in private."

Kobolowski spotted Claire from the back of the station and immediately rushed across the desks to alert Muldoon. "Yo, the Peterson woman is here," he whispered urgently.

Muldoon's eyes widened in panic. "Claire? Here? Why?"

"I don't know," Kobolowski replied. "But just listen to me —nah-thing. Say nah-thing. Silent treatment. Lack of communication. Got it?"

Claire approached the desk. "Hi, Danny. I thought I'd bring you a coffee this time."

Kobolowski stood behind her, mouthing *Nah-thing!* and gesturing wildly at his partner. Danny, whose face usually lit up at the sight of Claire, looked past her to Kobolowski, confused.

"I didn't have the intel on how you take it, so I got everything," she said with a teasing smile, trying to lighten the mood. Just like the time Danny brought her coffee, the cardboard tray Claire carried was overflowing with every conceivable coffee accompaniment the diner offered—sugars, Sweet'n Low, half-and-half, skim milk, almond milk, and an assortment of flavored creams. It was all there, a testament to her thoroughness—or perhaps, a subtle jab at Danny's past over-the-top generosity.

Kobolowski was still in the middle of his over-the-top mime, a full-body performance, when Claire glanced back. He froze mid-gesture, looking like a little kid caught with his hand elbow-deep in the cookie jar.

"Anyway," Claire turned back to Muldoon. "I wanted to apologize… about the other day… with Ben."

Muldoon stayed silent, remembering his partner's advice. Lack of communication. He's got this.

Claire's expression shifted, her patience wearing thin. "You do realize I get the silent treatment enough at home, right?"

Muldoon glanced over her shoulder at Kobolowski, who urged him with wide eyes to stay strong.

"Well," Claire sighed. "Enjoy your caffeinated beverage. I am sorry about the other day."

And with that, she was gone.

After a moment, a wave of regret washed over him.

Danny Muldoon messed up. He swore under his breath, then dashed after her, hoping he wasn't too late.

"I'm sorry about that," Muldoon said, catching up to Claire just as she reached her car.

"Me too," Claire replied, her irritation fading as she looked at him. He was too nice a guy—and honestly, too darn cute. She found herself as smitten as her teenage daughter Molly. Claire's eyes softened as they met his, and a warmth spread through her—a feeling she hadn't experienced in a very long time.

"Could we just sit and talk?" she asked.

Sit? Talk? *Talk!?*

His face went pale. If Danny Muldoon had his own list of the most terrifying things on Earth, it would be the following:

1. Spiders
2. Snakes
3. Heights
4. Sit and Talk to a Girl

The two of them sat on a nearby park bench, shaded by a huge oak tree. The bench creaked under their weight, its worn wood covered in carved initials of past lovers. Around them, the park was alive with activity: kids laughing and playing tag, dogs barking happily, joggers passing by with their earbuds in.

"I'm sorry, Danny. It's been really crazy lately, and I took it out on you," Claire said, the warmth of the morning sun bathing her weary eyes. She wished things could be different—more organized, more predictable, just… less difficult.

She turned to face him, concern etched across her features. "I'm getting pressure to relocate Andrew."

"But… but why?" he asked, stunned. "We're doing fine."

"I know," Claire reassured him. "Any luck at all with his mother?"

"No," Muldoon told her. "He has an uncle, but he's overseas doing some kind of private contracting for the military.

He and the father haven't talked in years. The mother was an only child. Both sets of parents have passed away. So, no grandparents, no aunts, no cousins. Nothing."

Claire sighed heavily. She knew it was out of her control at this point.

"Andrew is going to need more permanent care. If not with family, then with people who are certified," she told him. "I'm sorry, Danny, but it's protocol."

"Protocol," Muldoon repeated, the word heavy on his tongue. He looked away, genuinely sad. Sad for Andrew. Sad for himself. "He keeps asking about his father."

Claire nodded. "I know. I'm working on it. Some days I feel like I can't get out of my own way. It's always something."

She leaned back on the bench and stared up at the sky, searching for answers or guidance or a sign—something, anything. She took Nana May's advice and closed her eyes, breathing deeply in through her nose, out through her mouth. Still nothing.

"Unicorn notebooks and colored pens," she said with a sad kind of laugh. "I was organized in high school, wasn't I? I had everything planned: college, marriage, kids. Then one day my three-year-old suddenly stopped talking. I knew something was wrong; mothers just know. They told me it was regressive autism. Ben was trapped in a sort of neurological prison—like he just vanished."

She paused to collect herself and looked down at the swaying shadows of the leaves on the ground.

"My husband couldn't deal. Here was this accomplished physician—a man with degrees from top universities plastering his office wall, published papers filling medical journals —and he couldn't even communicate with his own son."

Muldoon didn't know what to say or how to help. Claire continued, trying to lighten the mood a bit.

"I should've known we were doomed from the start. We met when we were in school. I was a Loyola Jesuit schoolgirl, and he was a Johns Hopkins research nerd. Ben was just his convenient escape clause.

So he starts a new practice and a new family in California, and I'm stuck in Baltimore. I tried to make it work, enrolled Ben at Kennedy Krieger—the top school in the country for kids with autism. They started him on a round-the-clock regimen of speech and language therapies and behavioral therapies. He was sleeping maybe four hours a night. I was probably getting two or three, tops.

It was all taking its toll."

Muldoon could see she was hurting. "Must be nice to be back home, though. Your mom. Old friends."

"Yeah, well… I thought coming back to a small town could fix everything. It doesn't," she admitted sadly.

Muldoon nodded and said matter-of-factly, "Those plans didn't work out for James Wilden either."

They let that sit out there for a minute, both realizing the sad truth.

"My mother's been great," continued Claire. "But we don't exactly see eye to eye when it comes to Ben. She thinks if I just light candles and breathe in through my nose and out through my mouth, everything will be fine."

Muldoon laughed. "Ha. I remember your mom. She was always a bit out there. Can I ask? Why isn't Ben in school?"

"I had him in school for a while, but… he had behavioral issues and would lash out. I was pretty much told to put him in an institution." She looked to Muldoon, seeking his approval and trying to convince herself. "But, I figured, if he's happy? If he's not hurting himself? Who better to help him than his family, right?"

Muldoon wanted to take her hand, hold her, kiss her, anything to show her how much he cared. But he just nodded and continued to listen.

"I used to beat myself up. Did I miss something? Did I do something? Did I *not* do something? The world can be really cruel. Going places got to be difficult. Ben would draw stares in stores, restaurants. He looks fine, doesn't look like he has special needs... but, when he's behaving badly... well, clearly that's bad parenting, right? Control your son, right?"

She did her best to hold back her tears and her anger.

"I just got so tired of all the misconceptions and unwanted advice. Say your kid has cancer, and people line up to bring you dinners. But your kid acts up in the grocery store because he has a neuro-diverse condition? Everyone just thinks you're a terrible mother."

Muldoon's mood changed. He turned to face Claire and looked her in the eye because this was important.

"You're not a bad mother, Claire. You didn't just give up and leave."

There was a real bitterness in his voice. They both knew he was talking about Andrew's mother, Allison Wilden.

"Raising a family on your own," Muldoon told her. "Helping stray kids. Taking in stray dogs. Heck, you even help find lost dinosaurs."

That finally made them smile, and they both realized how badly they needed it.

"I just want these kids to see all the amazing possibilities that are ahead of them. Life is full of surprises, right? Like the coming attractions for their own incredible movie, you know?"

Muldoon smiled back at her. "Right."

Claire closed her eyes—Zen, Nana May style—and took a deep breath: in through the nose, out through the mouth.

"It's so hard trying to communicate with these kids. Some days it's like a wall I can't get through. And Ben... if he would just let me hug him—just once—that would be the greatest gift."

Muldoon spotted an opportunity. Remembering his "lessons" from Andrew, he channeled Billy Crystal in *When Harry Met Sally* and began to speak with a silly accent.

"Would you like to go to the movies with me tonight?"

Claire was totally confused. "What? Why... why are you talking like that?"

"*Would you like to...*" He stopped and went back to his own voice. "Sorry. Um, would you like to go to the movies with me tonight?"

Claire was a bit taken aback. "Oh. I...I don't think that's a good idea."

"I understand," Muldoon said, trying to mask his disappointment.

"No, Danny, it's just that…well, Ben has a routine and…"

"Sure. Some other time."

"Maybe we could do dinner?" Claire said.

Danny's eyes went wide, and his voice rose a full octave higher. "Do dinner?"

"Yeah. I could cook. My house."

"Dinner," Muldoon repeated the word, the terror in his voice palpable. "Sure. Um, dinner would be good."

Danny Muldoon just added Number Five to his 'Most Terrifying Things on Earth' list:

1. Spiders
2. Snakes
3. Heights
4. Sit and Talk to a Girl
5. Have Dinner with a Girl.

IN MULDOON'S SMALL, cluttered apartment, Andrew stood beside the AV cart, his fingers tracing the worn edges of a VHS cassette sleeve.

"Okay, so today's feature is Disney's *Bambi*," Andrew announced, his voice filling the small apartment. "It's about this young deer who loses his mom."

He paused, a flicker of recognition crossing his face as he thought about the parallels in his own life.

"Bambi makes friends with the other animals, learns skills to survive on his own, and even falls in love."

The television screen sparked to life, casting a soft glow across the room. Andrew turned to the person beside him, a mix of hope and uncertainty in his eyes.

"See," he said with a small smile. "Everything you need is in the movies."

In the flickering light of the television, Andrew began to realize that real life was far more complex than anything in the movies.

POLICE STATION

"Dinner?!" Kobolowski shouted at his partner. "I thought you said you were gonna go to the movies? Dinner means conversation. Talking. Chit-chat. Oh, you're screwed, Danny Boy."

"I know," Muldoon replied, his shoulders slumped, feeling as if he'd rather face spiders or snakes or have to find a seat in a high school cafeteria as a freshman new kid. Anything but this!

"Say nothing," Kobolowski advised firmly. "Nah-thing. Let her do all the talking."

"I can't do this. I'm gonna need some help," Muldoon said with desperation. He reached for the phone.

ACROSS TOWN, Skype was sitting alone in the Man Cave, engrossed in watching *Fast Times at Ridgemont High*.

His cell phone rang.

"Talk to me... Yo, *RoboCop*, what's up?... Nope, Andrew's not here... What? Really?! And she said yes?... No, no, I just thought... I can help... Yes, I'm serious! Ok. Ok. Take it easy, man. I'll be right over."

He looked back at the television, angry that he just missed a crucial scene.

"What happened?"

PETERSON HOUSE

Claire rushed around, frantically trying to tidy up the disheveled house. She scooped up plastic Lego pieces and toy dinosaurs, shoving them into a wicker basket and sliding it under the coffee table. The living room was a mess of scattered books, crumpled blankets, and mismatched cushions. She quickly fluffed the cushions and straightened the throw blankets, giving the room at least some semblance of order. Pausing to check her reflection in the hallway mirror, she smoothed down her hair and adjusted her blouse. For a moment, she saw herself in a different light—almost pretty, softer around the edges. She let out a heavy sigh, whispering to herself, "This is good, *right? Right?*"

There had been a few dates in the past, but nothing stuck. A couple of guys from work had shown interest. A coworker set her up on a blind date once, but it went nowhere when she found out the guy was a hardcore Republican. She met a guy at Starbucks who seemed nice—until she discovered he was married. Between her demanding job and Ben's strict schedule, any kind of meaningful relationship seemed impossible.

The kitchen timer beeped, pulling her from her thoughts. She hurried to pull out the lasagna she'd baked, hoping the smell might add a touch of warmth to the house.She set the tray back in for another fifteen minutes and glanced around one last time, trying to convince herself that everything would be okay. The house looked as presentable as it ever would, and for once, she felt a flicker of hope. Maybe this time, things would be different. Steadying herself, she prepared for what was to come. It had been years since she had dinner with an adult. Especially an adult male. Even more daunting was the fact that she kind of liked this particular adult male.The doorbell rang. She took one last deep breath then—"AAARGH!" she stepped on a sharp plastic Lego piece.

Great.

Perfect.

Standing on the front porch was Danny Muldoon, dressed in a cheesy retro powder blue tuxedo straight out of the 1980s. He was holding an enormous bouquet that seemed to contain every flower imaginable. Claire couldn't help but stifle a chuckle at the sight.

Muldoon was terrified. He cleared his throat nervously. "I, ah, I didn't have intel on your specific flower of choice... so, I requested all of them."

"Wow," Claire managed, struggling to hold the oversized bouquet in her hands. "Well, that certainly is quite a garden. You look... um, nice. I like your suit."

"Too much?" he asked, though Claire's expression told him all he needed to know. "I'm gonna kill that kid," Muldoon muttered through gritted teeth, more to himself than to Claire. This is the last time he takes advice from Skype!

"Make yourself at home. I just need to check on dinner," Claire said, gesturing for him to come inside.

As Muldoon wandered nervously through the living room, his fingers brushed past the books stacked on shelves and piled on the floor.

"You guys do a lot of reading, huh?" he remarked loudly enough for Claire to hear from the kitchen.

"We do," she shouted back, opening the oven door. "Molly especially."

"So, ah, where's your TV?"

"We don't have one," Claire yelled back.

Muldoon froze, panicked. He fumbled in his pocket for a DVD of *The Notebook*, wondering what to do next. *What the hell am I supposed to do now?*

Claire bounced back with two glasses of wine, interrupting his panic as Muldoon jammed the DVD case into his jacket.

"Come. Sit," Claire instructed him, motioning toward the couch. The dogs obediently settled beside them, but Muldoon struggled to find something to say, feeling like he was in a nightmare.

"So, um, no television at all, huh?" he finally broke the silence.

"No. Sorry. Did you want to watch something?" Claire asked innocently.

"Well, I thought we could…" Muldoon hesitated. Then, discreetly pulling out his trusty notepad, he read aloud, "Ah, '*Netflix and chill.*'"

Claire sputtered her wine, trying not to laugh.

"But since you don't have a TV, I guess we can just do the chill part."

"Do you even know what that means?" Claire asked playfully.

"Yes. Ah, no. No, not at all," Muldoon admitted, blushing.

Claire typed into her cell phone and then showed Muldoon the real meaning of '*Netflix and Chill.*' He was mortified.

"I'm gonna kill that kid!" he muttered through gritted teeth—again.

Claire smiled. "When Ben was young, he didn't like noise. For a while, we couldn't even have the lights on, so we got rid of the loud electronics like the TV. Molly fights me over it, but… you get used to the quiet. It's really kind of nice. We can just sit and talk."

"Sure. Just talk. Perfect," Muldoon echoed, feeling like he was living through his worst nightmare. They sat in an awkward silence, each equally uncomfortable.

"This is nice, *right? Right?*" Claire ventured, trying to break the tension.

Before Muldoon could even open his mouth, smoke exploded from the kitchen. The fire alarm shrieked a deafening BEEEEEP! Claire's eyes blew wide, and she was off like a shot.

MULDOON'S APARTMENT

"You have all that video equipment and you can't even work a microwave?!" Andrew yelled, his voice rough from fanning smoke out of their own burnt catastrophe a few miles away. He swatted at the haze turning Muldoon's tiny kitchen into a popcorn disaster zone.

"Don't blame me," Skype said, struggling to remove the batteries from a smoke alarm. "That thing is ancient." He was right. The microwave was enormous and old, like everything else in Muldoon's tired apartment. The faded wallpaper, threadbare carpet, and sagging furniture all spoke of a time when the place had been lovingly maintained by his mother, but now it just seemed sad and lonely.

Skype headed into the living room and plopped onto the worn Lay-Z-Boy recliner, grabbing the remote and flipping through channels.

CLICK.

"Gawd, I really am a loser," he said aloud.

CLICK.

"Saturday night. I'm eating burnt popcorn and watching a movie with a dude."

CLICK.

"At least I hooked my boy Muldoon up on his date though, right?"

CLICK.

"Wonder how that's going."

CLICK.

"There's never anything good on."

CLICK.

"I am so bored."

He glanced towards the adjacent bedroom, the door slightly ajar, revealing a meticulously made bed. "Yo, let's go see if he's got any 'cop stuff' in there. You know... like, contraband."

"Do you even know what contraband means?" asked Andrew.

"Yes. Ah, no. Not at all, actually," Skype admitted. "But let's see if we can find some anyway," he said, hopping out of the chair and racing across the room.

Stepping into Muldoon's mom's room was like entering a museum. The bed was pulled so taut you could practically play drums on it. Military awards and photos from her son's years in uniform covered the walls, and the dresser was perfectly organized, not a single item out of place. This was clearly a woman who ran a tight ship. Andrew shifted uncomfortably. "We shouldn't be in here."

"Come on. It's bad enough we're in on a Saturday night missing all the parties," Skype said, then he spotted a cardboard box marked EVIDENCE on the closet floor. It was the same one Kobolowski showed Muldoon at the station. "Yo! Jackpot!"

"I don't think this is a good idea," Andrew started, but it was too late. Skype was already tearing through the box. He yanked out a thick envelope, and a pile of photographs tumbled onto the perfectly made bed. Andrew's eyes widened with curiosity, his voice barely above a whisper. "That's... that's my mom."

He began to sift through old black-and-white photos and Polaroids. There were vacations at the beach, trips to the mountains, snapshots of Allison Wilden in New York, Rome, and Paris. His mother looked so young, beautiful, and carefree, a stark contrast to the mom he knew. Skype could see his friend's confusion and spoke up. "So, you guys traveled a lot, huh?"

Andrew stared at the photos, perplexed. "No," he said, his words measured and firm. "We never left the house."

Skype removed a lanyard with a glossy ID attached: PROFESSOR ALLISON HUGHES - NEW YORK UNIVERSITY.

"Hughes?" he asked.

"That was her maiden name," Andrew replied.

Andrew reached into the box and pulled out an old passport. Flipping through the pages, he stared at the stamps from Vietnam, Tokyo, Africa, and Iceland. It turned out Allison Hughes was a renowned film producer specializing in documentaries, her work taking her on adventures across the globe. It was a whole world and a whole life he never knew about his mother.

"Wow," Andrew muttered with a mixture of pride and envy. His finger traced a stamp from Ireland. "She's been everywhere."

The passport was like a window into a life full of adventure and excitement, far beyond the small town he knew.

"She made movies, huh?" asked Skype. "That's cool."

Andrew was momentarily speechless, reeling with each revelation, and meekly replied, "I guess." His mother had never shared anything about her happy, well-traveled life before being stuck in Medfield.

It's incredible what teenagers don't see. They're so busy being teenagers that they miss the bills stacking up in a wicker basket by the fridge or the laundry piled high by the machine. They don't realize their parents might be silently struggling with their choices. They never ask about hopes and dreams and happiness. It's not that they don't care; they just don't notice all the grown-up stuff. They're caught up in their own worlds, navigating the complexities of high school, friendships, and the latest trends, unaware of the weight their parents might carry every day. Andrew was starting to realize that he didn't really know his mother at all.

Skype reached back into the box and found a thick black ledger.

"That's from the store," Andrew told him. "My dad kept notes so he could make personal recommendations for every customer."

"Cool," replied Skype. "Sort of like an algorithm. *Netflix*, before *Netflix*."

"My dad, he knew every movie—all the lines and stuff," Andrew continued, staring at all his mother's photos and award certificates, trying to make some sense of it all. "But my mom... well, she's the one who taught me what the lines really meant."

Skype was busy reading the ledger.

"Oh. My. Gawd!"

"What?" asked Andrew.

"Dude. Best! Find! Ever!" Skype declared, his eyes wide with excitement. But Andrew wasn't listening—he was too busy looking at a manila folder he found at the bottom of the box titled: ALLISON WILDEN. He scanned Muldoon's paperwork, noting the multiple times he had tried to call her: No Answer. Left a Message. Voice Mail.

"Let's go," Andrew said firmly.

"What's in that folder?"

"I said let's go! Now!" he snapped, then angrily threw the folder back into the box.

PETERSON HOUSE

Claire fumbled with the oven mitts, yanking open the oven door to reveal a tray of lasagna engulfed in smoke.

"Dammit," she muttered, waving her hand to disperse the smoke. The smell of burnt cheese filled the room, and she coughed, reaching up to silence the blaring smoke alarm.

"Everything okay?" Muldoon called from the living room, his voice tinged with concern.

"Yep!" Claire replied, her voice strained as she tossed the charred remains into the sink. She turned on the faucet, letting water cascade over the blackened tray, steam hissing into the air. Taking a deep breath, she tried to regain her composure. The perfect evening she had envisioned was crumbling before her eyes. As she stared at the burnt meal smoldering in her sink, all Claire could do was laugh, pour an oversized glass of wine, and head back to the living room to join Muldoon, hoping to salvage this smoky disaster of a dinner date. She wiped her hands on a dishtowel and forced a smile as she re-entered the living room.

"Sorry about that," she said, her cheeks flushed.

Muldoon gave her a reassuring smile, the tension easing from his face. "We can always order pizza. They know me at Casa Bella. I'm kind of a regular there."

"Yeah, pizza sounds good," she chuckled, the sound helping to dispel some of the stress. "I got Ben settled back down. That alarm really upset him. I'm sorry about that," Claire said, trying to mask her worry.

"It's fine," Muldoon reassured her with a soft smile.

Claire sank into the couch as deeply as the cushion would let her, hoping she could just float away. "I had a beautiful dinner planned. I had everything planned," she sighed, her voice wavering. It had been a while since she cried, and she wasn't about to start now. Holding her glass of wine in the air, she gave a mock toast. *"Ladies and gentlemen, this is your Captain speaking. Welcome to Holland."*

Muldoon looked at her, confused. "Holland?"

Claire smiled a sad smile and tried to explain. "There was this article I read years ago. '*Welcome to Holland**.' I think every parent who has a kid with special needs knows it." She looked off and recited from memory.

"When you find out you're going to have a baby, it's like planning a fabulous trip to Italy. You buy a bunch of guidebooks and make your wonderful plans: the Colosseum, Michelangelo's David, the gondolas in Venice. It's all so exciting. And after months of anticipation, the day finally arrives, so you pack your bags and off you go. But when the plane lands, the pilot comes on and says, '*Welcome to Holland*.' What do you mean Holland? I'm supposed to be in Italy. All my life I've dreamed of going to Italy. But there's been a change in the flight plan. You landed in Holland."

---

*　*Welcome to Holland* by Emily Perl Kingsley. 1987

She picked up a plastic Lego piece from the end table beside her and stared at it.

"But they haven't taken you to a horrible, disgusting place; it's - it's just a different place. So, you have to go out and buy new guidebooks, learn a new language, meet a whole new group of people that you would never have met. And after you've been there for a while and you catch your breath, you look around - you begin to notice that Holland has windmills, and Rembrandts, and tulips."

She twirled the red plastic Lego between her fingers, her expression turning melancholy and reflective.

"But everyone you know is busy coming and going from Italy... and they're all bragging about what a wonderful time they had there. And you say, 'Yeah, that's where I was supposed to go.'"

Her body language shifted from sadness to resolution as she turned to face Muldoon.

"But if you spend your whole life sad that you didn't get to Italy, you'll never be free to enjoy all the beautiful tulips in Holland, *right? Right?*"

Muldoon totally got it. He gave her a soft, reassuring smile, then reached out and just took her hand. For a second, his touch was exactly the comfort and understanding she'd been desperate for.

"Do you know I've had a crush on you since high school?" Muldoon looked deeply into her eyes and confessed.

"Really?" Claire asked, a smile creeping onto her face.

"I think it was your unicorn notebook," he said with a smirk. "It's just... I never knew how to talk to you. I never knew how to talk to anybody."

Claire smiled. "Talking is so overrated."

Muldoon moved in close, his heart pounding like a drum. Claire closed her eyes, eagerly awaiting his kiss, feeling the warmth of his breath mingling with hers. The world around them seemed to disappear, leaving only the electricity of anticipation hanging in the air. Then… "AAAH!" Muldoon yelped in pain and pulled a sharp Lego piece from under his hip.

The sudden noise made Ben cry out from his room. Claire shot Muldoon an apologetic look, then practically flew to check on her son. And just like that, the moment was gone.

MEDFIELD

Andrew and Molly settled into a cozy, retro diner, a jukebox softly humming oldies in the background. They shared a milkshake with two straws between them, their heads close together as they re-enacted the iconic scene with Danny Zuko and Sandy Olsson from *Grease*. The soft glow of the neon washed over their faces, and the distant scent of burgers and fries just made the whole place feel super nostalgic. Molly smiled warmly. "I've had so much fun on these dates, Andrew. Thank you."

Andrew looked her in the eye and quoted, *"Life moves pretty fast. If you don't stop and look around once in a while, you could miss it."*

Molly was mesmerized. "You know, most high school kids, all they ever do is try to be someone else," she said. "But not you. You're so unique and original."

Andrew couldn't help but feel a tinge of guilt knowing that none of the ideas were his own. This whole time, he hadn't been himself. Instead, he had been hiding behind the personas of his favorite movies: Emilio Estevez, Matthew Broderick, Judd Nelson. The way they carried themselves, the lines they delivered effortlessly, the ease with which they navigated life—Andrew had borrowed all of it. He felt more comfortable being someone else than facing the world as Andrew. He knew it was wrong, but at the moment, he didn't care. He was having too much fun to let it bother him. And besides, Molly didn't know.

"Tell me about your old school," Molly asked, her curiosity piqued. "What was it like?"

Andrew squirmed in his seat a little. "Well, um, it was... it was a lot smaller. We only had, like, a few students."

Molly looked a bit confused but was so smitten with Andrew that she didn't care. She looked off and wondered aloud, "Maybe it was the kind of school that didn't have rules. Maybe it was the kind of school where people were nice to each other and didn't care about 'status' and 'likes' and 'followers.' No *Plastics*, or *Jocks*, or *Freaks* and *Nerds*. Just kids. Just people—people who actually talk with each other. Does a school like that even exist? Do people like that even exist?"

"Maybe in the movies," Andrew answered.

"Maybe," she said matter-of-factly. "I certainly wouldn't know."

Molly glanced toward the small, dusty TV perched in the corner of the diner, flashing silently.

"If I had a TV, maybe I could be 'normal.' Maybe I could sit at the cool table and talk about the latest reality show instead of reading actual books. But we didn't choose to live that way. We chose to protect Ben."

Silence filled the space between them as Molly's honesty hung in the air. "I know I resent him for it sometimes. For making us... different. I just thought high school was going to be... different."

Her eyes began to glisten with soft tears. "But that first week of school, watching them... watching her... I learned what lonely felt like. Like, really lonely."

Andrew knew exactly how she felt.

The bells jingled above the diner's front doorway, and Andrew immediately looked up out of habit.

"Why do you always do that?" Molly asked, noticing his reaction. "Whenever we're out, you always look up when you hear bells."

After a moment of searching for an answer, Andrew confessed. "We had bells like that in my dad's store. Every time someone entered, they would jingle, and I'd look up, thinking maybe it was my mother. For a while, I really thought she'd come back. But it was never her. It was just families, coming and going as they pleased."

There was real jealousy in his voice. His words became measured and firm.

"Eventually, I started hating the sound of those bells," Andrew said, his eyes rising to meet Molly's across the table. "And lately… I realized my mom did too."

Molly's eyes lingered on the boy across from her. He was no longer just Andrew; he was mature, confident, resolved.

Andrew tried to think of something clever or witty to say, but his mind came up blank. So, he reached for her hand instead. Molly grasped it tightly, her fingers pressing into his like someone clinging to the edge of a cliff. He gasped at the sudden sharpness, but when she realized and relaxed her grip, looking embarrassed, Andrew responded by gently squeezing her hand back. They both smiled.

Suddenly, the bells jingled again as another customer entered, but this time Andrew jokingly locked his gaze on Molly, trying his best not to look up.

"Yo! *Whaddup*, guys?" a familiar voice boomed. The special moment was broken when Skype suddenly popped his head between them.

"Oh, hey, Skype," Molly smiled. "You want to join us?"

Andrew drilled him with a look. Skype got the not-so-subtle hint.

"No. No, it's cool. I'll just sit over here - leave you two lovebirds alone," he said, sliding into the booth behind them.

Molly and Andrew went back to their milkshake.

"Thanks for sharing, you know, about your mom," Molly said.

"My mom… she was really smart," Andrew told her. "Home-schooled me in everything. Math. Social studies. Even taught me how to dissect a penguin."

"Stop that. She did not," Molly laughed. After a moment, she confessed softly, "I think that's when I realized that I liked you."

Andrew tried to concentrate, but all he could focus on was that she liked him.

"What I meant was that I studied them," he continued. "Emperor penguins, actually. My dad showed me how they attract a mate by singing a unique 'heartsong.' If the male penguin's heartsong matches the female's song, then they become mates."

Molly reached across the table and took both his hands in hers.

"I mean, my dad's heart was always in the right place. He was just kind of, I don't know... different. Then after my mother left," he looked away for a moment. "I could tell things weren't right. He got more paranoid, more protective, more restricted."

Molly could see that he was struggling. She squeezed his hand, gave a knowing, warm smile, and said, *"We're all pretty bizarre. Some of us are just better at hiding it, that's all."*

Andrew smiled back, still feeling guilty, so he switched gears to lighten the mood.

"My mom was sweet, but tough, you know? This one time, she took in a homeless teenager from the rough side of the tracks. He couldn't read but was great at football."

"Really?" Molly said, confused but impressed.

"Yeah. She was a huge football fan," Andrew continued with newfound bravado. "And the kid, well, the kid was huge, too. He saved my life one time in a car crash."

Skype was listening from the booth behind them. He slouched down and rolled his eyes as Andrew continued his made-up story.

"That's amazing," said an enamored Molly, then noticed the clock on the wall. "Oooh, jeez. I gotta go."

She leaned in, whispered, "You are amazing," then surprised Andrew with a kiss on the cheek. Andrew beamed as he watched Molly hurry off.

Skype slid into her empty seat.

"Homeless youth? Football player? Car crash? You never

told me your mother was Sandra Bullock from *The Blind Side*. You better make sure Molly never sees that movie."

"It's fine," replied Andrew with a way-too-cocky smirk. "I have a better chance of her seeing your *YouTube* movies. As in, it's never gonna happen."

Skype winced because that stung.

Andrew exuded a newfound swagger, bordering on outright cockiness that reminded Skype of that arrogant, testosterone-fueled bully, Ricky Sherman.

MEDFIELD HIGH SCHOOL

Mr. Gleason was in a particularly bad mood. His psoriasis and rosacea seemed angrier than usual, making his face look like it was about to burst into flames.

"Find your seats, ladies and gentlemen," he commanded. "Today!"

The class rushed to settle in, chairs scraping against the floor and backpacks slung onto desks. Ricky "accidentally" bumped into Andrew, sending his books tumbling and scattered to the floor. The class giggled, some whispering behind their hands. Ricky leaned over, his face inches from Andrew's, and growled, "Don't forget who runs things around here."

Skype quickly bent down to help his friend retrieve the scattered books, sensing Andrew's boiling rage.

"Let's go, Mr. Wilden!" Gleason barked at Andrew, then faced the students with a sheet of paper in his hand. "Alright, which brilliant young mind handed this in? There's no name on it. You, Miss Standish? Mr. Clark? Ah, of course... Mr. Sherman."

Ricky sat up from his slouched position, "That's not mine. I didn't..."

"You didn't what, Mr. Sherman? Read the assignment? That's painfully obvious. Do I need to remind you all of the upcoming mid-term?"

Ricky glanced at his Sidekicks with a reassuring smirk, silently communicating, *'we got this.'*

Gleason's rant continued. "Is anyone paying attention? It's all right here in the book, people. Just read."

The class was tense with fear. Molly bravely raised her hand. "I read the book, Mr. Gleason. I thought..."

"You thought?" snapped Gleason. "What did you *think*, Miss Peterson?"

"I... I just thought you might appreciate a different perspective" she explained tentatively. "Something more... original."

"Original? You were off-topic, Miss Peterson," Gleason replied mockingly, searching for her paper. "Judgmental. Overly opinionated. The syllabus was created for a reason. Just stick to the subject matter and give me what I ask for, Miss Peterson."

Molly's shoulders slumped, and she sank deeper into her seat, as if trying to disappear into it and escape the room altogether. Andrew had seen enough. With a loud, muffled cough, he yelled out, "Eat me."

The class fell into stunned silence. Mr. Gleason visibly struggled to contain his rage. His face turned a darker shade of red, veins bulging on his forehead.

"What? Who... who said that?" he demanded, his voice trembling with fury.

"*You gonna bark all day, little doggie... or are you gonna bite?*" Andrew calmly replied. Mr. Gleason was on the brink of exploding. "Wilden?!"

"*Hey bud, what's your problem?*" Andrew replied coolly, meeting the teacher's furious gaze head-on.

"Are you out of your mind?!" Gleason snapped.

Andrew remained unfazed. He stared directly at the teacher and delivered his next line with cutting precision. "*You are a sad, strange little man. And you have my pity.*"

The class was in utter shock. Mouths hung open and eyes widened in disbelief. No one said a word. Not one word.

Molly leaned over to Andrew, her voice a frantic whisper. "Stop. You're going to get in trouble."

But Andrew was calm and defiant. "*Frankly, my dear, I don't give a damn.*"

Gleason was seething. It wasn't just his rosacea or psoriasis acting up; it was pure anger, driving his blood pressure to dangerously high levels.

"I'm not going to take this from some... some home-schooled savant!" Gleason exclaimed.

Suddenly, the sharp shriek of chair legs on the tiled floor broke the tension as Skype bolted up from his seat.

"Sit down, Mister Johnson," Gleason ordered sharply, his eyes burning with fury.

But Skype remained standing, ready to defend his friend.

"Do you have any idea where this 'home school' was, Mr. Gleason?" Skype asked with a newfound air of confidence.

"I said sit down!" Gleason commanded—but it was no use; he'd lost all control.

"*COMING ATTRACTIONS* video store. Ever heard of it?" Skype said with a smirk.

Gleason was visibly shaken. The whole class could see it. He blinked a few times, his train of thought derailed as he took a deep breath as if trying to restrain himself. Skype reached into his backpack and pulled out the thick black ledger from the box in Muldoon's apartment.

"Apparently, you were quite a regular back in the day," Skype announced calmly, scanning the pages like a lawyer grilling a witness. He looked up from the notebook, his eyes narrowing as he studied his teacher's reaction. "Let's see here. 'Vernon Gleason.' Ah, here it is. You rented *Titanic* eight times."

"'I'm so cold, Jack,'" Andrew mimicked in a high-pitched voice.

The class giggled. Skype continued to read the ledger. "*Twilight*. You rented that eleven times."

"'*Hold on tight, spider monkey*,'" Andrew mocked.

Nervous laughter filled the room. Skype was loving every minute of this.

"Hmmmm," he continued. "Ah, *Sisterhood of the Traveling Pants*. Fifteen rentals."

Howls of laughter erupted from the classroom. Gleason was reeling, his knees buckling as he stumbled backward, collapsing into his chair. His face flushed with deep embarrassment as the laughter echoed around him.

"And of course," continued Skype, "that wonderful tale of one magical summer at a sleepy resort in the Catskills – *Dirty Dancing*. You rented that video a store record thirty-seven times."

The room exploded with laughter. Gleason wanted to die. Andrew took the ledger from Skype and approached the front desk.

"'*Nobody puts Baby in a corner...*' Vern," Andrew said, letting the ledger fall hard onto Gleason's lap in the most humiliating mic drop move ever.

Skype and Andrew high-fived each other. For a moment, Molly thought they resembled Ricky's sidekicks, high-fiving whenever he did something cool – and she wasn't sure what to make of this newfound air of confidence. Andrew turned to the class before heading out the door and said with a cocky grin, "'*There's a new sheriff in town. Y'all be cool.*'"

As they walked out the door, Skype caught sight of Vernon's expression. He looked small and deflated, completely drained of authority, like a peacock who'd just been plucked of all its feathers. For a moment, he almost felt sorry for him.

In the back of the room, Ricky Sherman sat steaming—as angry and red and homicidal as his humiliated Social Studies teacher.

PETERSON HOUSE

"Hey guys," Claire greeted the dogs as she bent down to pet

them. "I had to come home to get something. Has anyone seen a folder on Andrew Wilden? Mom? Hello?"

No response.

She walked into Ben's playroom, which was full of Legos and plastic dinosaurs, but it was empty. '*That's odd*,' she thought, and headed upstairs.

"Molly, where's your brother?" she asked, poking her head into her daughter's bedroom.

"I just got home," Molly replied, reading at her desk. "Isn't he with Nana May?"

A sudden rush of panic washed over Claire. She hurried down to the kitchen.

"Mom, where's Ben? Mom?"

Nana May was quietly meditating, surrounded by candles, and couldn't hear over the loud Joni Mitchell music.

"Mom?!"

Nana May snapped out of her deep trance. "What...? Why are you home so early?"

"Where is Ben, Mom?" Claire asked, a tangible panic rising in her voice.

"Don't be mad," Nana May replied sheepishly.

"Where is he?"

After a moment, Nana May admitted, "He's... he's with Danny Muldoon. At his apartment."

Claire was visibly shaken. "What?! Why?"

"Let me explain," Nana May pleaded.

But Claire was already out the door.

MULDOON'S APARTMENT

"Where is Ben?" Claire nearly screamed as she burst past Muldoon into his apartment.

"Claire? I... I can explain," Muldoon stammered, standing by the open door.

"You have no right to take my son."

"I... I thought it might be good for him to get out."

"You thought?!" Claire's eyes blazed with fury.

"Will you just let me talk for a second?" Muldoon said firmly, trying to calm her. His tone finally made Claire pause. She took a deep breath, giving him a chance to explain.

"Okay, now listen," he began cautiously. "A couple of weeks ago, I went by your house looking for Andrew. I was taking him to the Franklin Park Zoo since he's never been. Andrew wasn't there, so your mom asked if I'd take Ben instead."

"She what?!" Claire interrupted.

"I know, but your mom said Ben had never been there either." Muldoon hesitated, knowing his next words might hurt. "She said he'd never been anywhere, actually."

Claire bit her lip, allowing him to continue.

"We came back to my place to get Andrew, and he was here watching a movie on TV. I can't remember what it was. Anyway, Ben's face lit up. He was captivated, laughing, repeating the lines. I couldn't get him to leave."

Claire looked at Ben, who was sitting across the room quietly watching an animated Disney movie on the television. He seemed calm, not stimming, content.

Muldoon spoke up again. "We've been coming back almost every afternoon. Last week he and Andrew watched *Bambi*. You said Ben needs a routine." He paused, choosing his words carefully. "It's not good for anyone to live a lonely, socially isolated life."

The words hung in the air, drifting around and landing on everyone in the room. Loneliness meant something different to each of them, and it felt as though the walls were closing in. For a moment, everything else just disappeared. Claire was still struggling to grasp the depth of it all, her mind racing.

"I'm sorry," Muldoon continued. "I should have told you. I just thought it might be good because…"

"Because why?" Claire snapped, her voice cracking. "Because he's so unhappy? Because I'm a bad mother? Because…"

Suddenly, a voice cut across the room.

"Because he needs to leave the house!"

Claire and Muldoon turned to see Andrew, his voice so stern it surprised them both.

"My father thought he was doing the right thing, creating a kind of bubble to keep us safe in our own world," Andrew confided, his voice tinged with a mix of sadness and frustration. "We lived a sheltered life. Dad downstairs, buried in his world of movies, Mom upstairs homeschooling me. I only had movie characters for friends and played out scenes in my head." Andrew's voice softened, the pain evident. "I missed out on all the normal stuff. Birthday parties, school dances, just hanging out with kids my own age. All those little things that make you feel alive." He looked at Claire, his face softening a bit. "I know you mean well, trying to protect Ben, but life is about experiencing things. My dad tried to shield us, thinking it would keep us safe from the world. But in the end, all he did was tear us apart."

Andrew looked at Ben, then back to Claire. "You need to let him find his way. You need to let him be part of the world."

Then, in a voice just barely above a whisper, Ben spoke, "*Just like Ariel.*"

Claire turned, stunned. It was like a lightning bolt hit the room. It was the first time she'd heard her son speak in years.

"Did... did you say something, Ben?"

"Just like Ariel," Ben repeated, his eyes never leaving *The Little Mermaid* playing on the TV.

Claire's head was spinning. She looked at Ben in disbelief, then turned to Muldoon for answers. "I... I don't understand."

"I read about a family in Boston," Muldoon explained. "They had a son like Ben who stopped talking when he was about three. He started watching Disney films and would act out the characters. He didn't just mimic them; he seemed to understand and relate to their emotions. The family started speaking to him in the characters' voices, and it worked. He eventually came out of his shell, and they found a way to communicate again."

"I… I don't know what to say," Claire said, her lip trembling, tears welling in her eyes.

Muldoon glanced over at Andrew. "It was all his idea."

Claire didn't know what to say. She knelt beside her son, looking into his eyes as he continued to watch the movie, gently rocking back and forth. He seemed different—content, happy. There was an awakening in Ben of sorts. He was in the world.

Then Claire did something she hadn't done in what felt like forever. Slowly, gently, she reached out and wrapped an arm around Ben's small shoulders and hugged her son—and he let her.

MEDFIELD HIGH SCHOOL

Skype and Andrew stood by their lockers as the three *Plastics* sauntered down the hallway. There was a monumental shift. Everything changed. Everyone—not just the freshman class, but upperclassmen too—heard about what had happened. How Andrew had totally embarrassed Mr. Gleason.

"Hey guys," Plastic 1 called out.

Skype and Andrew did a double-take to make sure she was actually speaking to them.

"We heard about what happened the other day in Mr. Gleason's class," added Plastic 2. "Super cool."

"We're having a party Saturday night," Plastic 3 told them. "You guys should come."

Skype almost lost it. "Us guys? Like, him and me? Really?"

"Yeah. Sure," replied Plastic 1, granting his wish like a queen from her throne. The Plastics went back to their all-too-important iPhone texting and sauntered away down the hall.

Skype turned to Andrew, his jaw almost hitting the floor. It took him a minute to process it all. "Did…did that just happen?" he asked, physically placing his jaw shut. "Did we just get invited to a party? A high school party? I've lived in this town for fifteen years and have never been invited to anything! Cameron Broderick's pool party. Jake Schoeffling's Bar Mitzvah. Nancy Ringwald's birthday party at Applebee's —although everyone got food poisoning, so, yep, kinda glad I missed that one. But, holy shit, bro, we're going to a party! With girls and beer and girls and music and girls! Did I mention girls? I think I did, didn't I?" He took a breath and talked himself down. "Ok. Be cool, bro. Be cool. We are so in, brother," he smiled and gave Andrew a rousing high five.

"'*You can be my wingman anytime,*'" smirked Andrew.

Skype smiled back. "'You can be mine.'"

MEDFIELD HIGH SCHOOL

Walking through the halls the next morning on his way to the lockers, everything was different. There was a bounce in Andrew's step—a happiness and excitement that radiated from him. Where he usually walked with his head down, trying to avoid being seen, today he walked with his head held up, smiling, laughing, high-fiving, and dapping passing students. The bustling hallways of Medfield High seemed a little brighter, a little more welcoming, as if they, too, could sense the change in him.

He smiled as he spun the combination lock, feeling the click of each number under his fingers. It opened with ease! Andrew was finally getting the hang of things around here. Today was going to be a good day. He smiled and closed the locker door to see—Mr. Gleason, red-faced and furious as ever, standing on the other side.

"Mister Wilden," he said with an ominous tone. "They'd like to see you in Principal Shepherd's office. Now."

THE SCHOOL OFFICE was strategically positioned at the heart of the main building, sandwiched between the library and the bustling cafeteria, and directly opposite the student center. There were glass walls reaching halfway up, giving an unobstructed view so that any students passing by could easily see who was in trouble.

Outside Principal Shepherd's office sat Mrs. Scully, a woman so ancient she might have been present for the very first day of school—ever. She looked like she was somewhere between eighty and one hundred and eighty, with a grumpy disposition that suggested she'd been through more school years than anyone could count. Her desk was a masterpiece of disorganization. The computer screen was buried under a mountain of yellow sticky notes—urgent reminders for the perpetually overworked receptionist to order more supplies. Her twisted, arthritic fingers tapped the keyboard with a kind of resigned precision, as if she were playing a dreary, never-ending game of "hunt and peck." It was clear from her audible sighs and irritated mutters that Mrs. Scully had long since given up pretending to enjoy her job.

Andrew slumped in the chair opposite Mrs. Scully, awaiting his fate. He scanned the room, his eyes drifting to the wall behind her. Three framed posters stared back at him: a snowy peak, a boundless ocean, and a fiery sunset. Beneath each one, a single, bold word: MOTIVATION, CHAL-LENGE, PERSISTENCE. Just like the cheesy "Bumper Sticker Philosophy" posters in Claire's office, he thought. Did these come standard with every school office? Were they some kind of universal memo, designed to magically inspire trou-bled teens? He seriously doubted it.

Andrew stared up at the posters plastered on the wall. They were clearly meant to inspire young minds, but all he could think about was how he'd probably see the same posters years from now, hanging in some dull office cubicle or staff lounge, urging exhausted adults to stay motivated as they slogged through their daily grind. He imagined himself, burdened with a mortgage, college loans, and car payments, staring at those posters and feeling just as disillusioned as Mrs. Scully, the overworked receptionist, or Mr. Costello, the miserable janitor he'd passed earlier, cleaning up a rancid spill outside the cafeteria. These were the people who kept things running—marginalized, everyday workers who were so under-appreciated by everyone.

Andrew knew he had plenty of time to worry about that stuff later. Right now, he just wanted to enjoy being a kid— really enjoy it. Being a teenager can suck. High school is the worst. But not to Andrew. The Plastics, the Jocks, the Basket Cases, the Nerds—he wanted to experience it all, maybe even make one or two friendships that would last. Wasn't that what being a teenager was supposed to be about? Isn't that what life was all about?

Mrs. Scully stood at her desk and left for a moment. Andrew smirked ever so slightly. He reached for a nearby Sharpie pen and drew a thick black line through the posters, replacing the words *MOTIVATION*, *CHALLENGE*, and *PERSISTENCE*, and scribbling in their place *SMILE*, *RELAX*, *ENJOY*.

Andrew sat back, pleased with himself and his new super-cool status at Medfield High. But the satisfaction was short-lived. The door to Principal Shepherd's office swung open, and Andrew's stomach tightened. He could see that Claire Peterson was inside. Something serious was happening.

PRINCIPAL SHEPHERD, a heavyset man with thick black glasses and a comb-over that defied gravity, sat in his dark, wood-paneled office. The walls were lined with diplomas and certificates, each one proudly displayed as if to say, "Look at all the degrees I've earned but can't quite make this hair look normal." Inspirational quotes were everywhere, ranging from the overly sentimental to the eye-roll-inducing, like *"Dream*

Big," "*Success Is Not an Option*," and "*You Miss 100% of the Shots You Don't Take*." The bookcase was filled with self-help books, and Andrew wondered if any of them had ever been opened, or if they were just there for show. The whole room had the air of someone who took their job way too seriously. It was pretty clear to Andrew that Principal Shepherd was the one who ordered all the posters for the school.

"Is this about what happened in Mr. Gleason's class?" Andrew began. "Because I can explain."

"No, Andrew," Principal Shepherd said with a solemn gaze. He removed his glasses and then looked at Claire, signaling her to take it from here.

"There's been a change, Andrew," she began, her voice faltering. There was a sadness in her eyes that seemed to weigh heavily in the room. "A house just opened up in the city …"

Andrew's heart sank. "Is this because of Ben?" he interjected anxiously. "I was just trying to help."

Claire met his gaze, her expression pained. "No, Andrew. What you did… I could never thank you enough. But there are rules… protocol… and, well, this woman is certified."

The news hit Andrew like a gut punch. He felt his whole body tense with frustration and anger. "Did Molly and Skype know about this?"

Claire's voice was barely above a whisper. "I'm sorry. It was supposed to be temporary."

The word hit Andrew like a hammer. *Temporary.* Like a rental. Like one of the video cassettes from his father's store, passed from house to house, exchanged between families and friends, but never staying in one place for too long. He felt like the kitten hanging from the branch in Claire's office poster that read *Hang in There!*

Hang in there? How can I hang in there when I've got nothing and no one? Andrew thought. Then it hit him that he was about to be moved again, and burning anger surged through every part of him.

MEDFIELD HIGH SCHOOL

The Plastics sat at their usual table in the cafeteria, heads bent over their phones like they were decoding secret messages. They were texting so fast it looked like their thumbs might actually catch fire. Every so often, one of them glanced up and gave a dramatic eye roll, as if the rest of the world were just background noise to their endless chat threads. It was like a scene straight out of an old-fashioned, bad teen drama— nothing ever changed, except maybe the brand of lip gloss.

"Guys, my mom made me watch this wicked old movie the other night," Plastic 1 said as she turned the screen to show the others. "I thought I'd hate it, but—check this guy out. He is super cute."

"Oh, my gawd," screeched Plastic 2. "This is, like, my mom's favorite movie."

Plastic 3 nodded in agreement. "Oh my gawd. I think that guy's married to Sarah Jessica Parker from *Sex and the City*. This movie is from, like, the '80s."

Plastic 1 rolled her eyes. "The '80s? That's, like, forever ago. Did they even make movies back then?"

Plastic 2 and Plastic 3 laughed. That was part of their job description—to laugh whenever Plastic 1 said something even mildly amusing.

Molly was sitting at the table behind them, quietly reading, but she couldn't help overhearing the conversation. She spoke up.

"The '80s were a pretty cool decade, actually. Some great music."

They looked in her direction. *Really?*

"The clothes back then were super bright. You three would certainly love it," Molly said, a bit of sarcasm in her voice. "My mother wore a bright pink dress to her high school prom."

Plastic 1 suddenly had an idea, like it was the first time

ever. "That's it, guys!" she exclaimed. "The prom! We should do an '80s theme."

"Totally," replied Plastic 3. "My mom has cool costume jewelry. We could do all neon and, like, super old music."

Plastic 1 clapped her hands, reclaiming her role as the leader. "We need to get to work on this right away. Neon clothes, big hair, and the best '80s hits. It's going to be epic!"

Plastic 2 nodded eagerly. "I'll start looking for the perfect dress. And we can get those colorful bracelets and leg warmers."

Plastic 1 turned her attention back to the movie playing on her phone.

"Ooh, this is, like, my favorite part," she said, turning up the volume on her phone. Words flowed out from the tiny speaker:

"*'Life moves pretty fast. If you don't stop and look around once in a while, you could miss it.'*"

Suddenly, Molly was standing behind them, staring at the screen of their iPhone. The look on her face said it all—surprise, confusion, hurt. Her eyes widened and her mouth hung open, as if she couldn't believe what she was seeing. She seemed frozen in place, her shoulders tense. It was clear that whatever she saw on that screen had changed everything.

"I know this," she said with a puzzled look.

"You?" asked Plastic 1. "You've seen this movie?"

"Wait, I thought you didn't have a TV," Plastic 3 said, filled with surprise.

Molly kept staring at the phone. "We don't. But I... I heard that somewhere."

The Plastics looked at each other knowingly and giggled. "Maybe she should ask her boyfriend. He's seen, like, every movie ever."

They laughed among themselves. Plastic 1 scribbled something on a piece of paper and handed it to Molly.

"Here," she said with a sly smirk. "Google this."

Molly walked away in total confusion, staring at the note in her hand.

MULDOON'S APARTMENT

The bedroom was thick with tension as Andrew packed his duffel bag. Every shirt, every pair of jeans he jammed into his duffel bag was a silent shout, heavy with all the things he couldn't say. The only sounds were the rustle of fabric and the dull thud of his sneakers bumping against the buckles, each one a punctuation mark in the raging silence.

"So, ah, you sure you got everything?" asked Muldoon, trying to help.

No response.

"Claire said this lady is really nice."

Still nothing.

"You don't have to do this," Andrew finally replied firmly.

"Do what?" asked Muldoon.

"Pretend like you care," Andrew snapped, the anger and hurt in his voice hitting Muldoon like a punch. "I found that box in your room," he said. "Saw the report. The manila folder with her name on it? It said you left my mom a ton of messages."

Muldoon froze. He didn't know how to respond.

"I… I was going to tell you, but…" Muldoon stopped. He knew he needed to tell Andrew the truth. "Yes, Andrew. We did locate the subject. Mrs. Wilden. I mean, your mother. She has yet to respond. I'm sorry."

Muldoon's cell phone buzzed.

Claire.

He ignored it.

Andrew finished packing. "Here, I don't need this," he said, tossing a Red Sox cap from their happy night at Fenway Park onto the bed. "I don't need anything."

Muldoon stood alone in the room, a mix of anger, confusion, and sadness churning inside him. He reached into his back pocket and pulled out a glossy pamphlet, staring at the words *Massachusetts Foster Care Application*. With a frustrated sigh, he tossed it onto the bed, where it landed next to the Red Sox hat.

His cell phone buzzed again.

Claire.

He stared at her name, a knot tightening in his stomach, before slamming his thumb down and turning the phone off.

BOSTON, MA

Andrew and Claire stood on the front steps of a drab, sad house, the duffel bag of clothes hanging over his shoulder. The odor of cigarettes and kitty litter wafted through the air, making Andrew feel dizzy. The house looked like it had seen better days, with peeling paint and a yard that needed tending. Claire gave Andrew a reassuring smile, but the worry in her eyes was unmistakable.

"This will be good, *right? Right?* Boston City High School, home of the Pirates. *Aaarrrgh!*" Claire said, trying to make the best of it, her voice pitched a little higher than usual.

Andrew was having none of it.

The door creaked open, revealing Mrs. O'Hara, a plain, older woman with kind eyes and a warm smile. Her hair was streaked with gray, pulled back into a neat bun. She wore a simple floral dress and an apron, looking like a grandmother from a storybook. But Andrew saw none of that. His eyes were fixed on the ground, lost in his own thoughts.

"You must be Andrew. So nice to meet you."

Andrew said nothing. He didn't even look up.

Claire stepped in to help. "I'm Claire Peterson. We spoke on the phone."

"Yes, of course," said Mrs. O'Hara, escorting them in. The house was as tired inside as it was outside; only the odor of cigarettes and kitty litter was stronger.

Claire attempted to put on a brave face. "This is nice. Isn't this nice, Andrew?"

Silence.

This was her cue to leave. She turned to Mrs. O'Hara. "Well, um… we can finalize all the paperwork Monday."

Claire peeked back through the window at Andrew. To her, he looked like a little boy—overwhelmed, lonely, sad, but mostly… angry. His shoulders were hunched, and his face was a mix of emotions she couldn't fully decipher. The weight of the world seemed to rest on him, and she felt helpless.

ANDREW SURVEYED HIS NEW ROOM. There was a bed with a plain navy-blue comforter, a nightstand cluttered with old magazines, and atop a worn brown oak dresser sat an old Zenith TV with rabbit-ear antennas sticking out at odd angles. The walls were bare, except for a few faded patches where posters used to hang. Andrew wondered if Principal Shepherd had sent some motivational ones to Mrs. O'Hara. The place was sparse, unfamiliar, and felt nothing like home.

"Not sure if the television works, but you can feel free to try," Mrs. O'Hara offered, trying to be helpful. "Well, I'll let you get settled in."

Andrew dropped his duffel bag in the corner, then sat on the edge of the bed and stared at the TV. He reached into his pocket for the black remote control that had belonged to his father and aimed it at the old Zenith. It didn't work. Of course it didn't. Nothing worked!

Things used to work, though—before. Before his mother left. Before his father had a breakdown. Before everything in his life changed. Before he became nothing but a problem. A temporary rental.

He slid the remote back into his pocket, opened the bedroom window, and ran off into the night.

Chapter 3

PETERSON HOUSE

It had been a long day, and Claire was emotionally exhausted. Moving Andrew had taken its toll. She quietly entered Ben's room to check on her sleeping son. The room was dim, lit only by the soft glow of a nightlight shaped like a dinosaur. She walked gingerly in her bare feet, trying to avoid the scattered toys on the floor. Suddenly, she stepped on the sharp edge of a Lego piece and muffled a scream: "MMMmnpph-haaargh!" Her face contorted in pain as she hopped on one foot, biting her lip to keep from waking Ben.

Perfect. Just perfect.

She sat on the edge of the bed and whispered, talking more to herself than to her son.

"Did you have a good day? I had a tough one. We had to relocate Andrew. He's not talking to me. Danny's not talking to me. Molly won't talk to me until we get a television. And you? Well, we're working on it, *right? Right?*"

She leaned down and gently brushed a strand of hair from Ben's forehead before pulling the blanket up a little higher.

The room was quiet, except for the soft hum of the night outside, and Claire felt the loneliness of the day settle in around her.

"Anything you wanna talk about? I don't know, like, maybe how you secretly hate Legos? How these little plastic pieces of pain always seem to find the bottom of my feet?" She twirled the small, bright red Lego brick between her fingers. "You look everywhere, trying to pick up the pieces, but there's always one you missed, you know? And you just can't seem to get your life organized." She gave a heavy, weighted sigh.

"And love? Don't even get me started. It's like I'm constantly searching for that missing Lego piece, the one that finally completes the set—but it's always just out of reach. Or worse, I find a piece I think will fit and then realize it's from a completely different box. Like it's married, or lives out of its car, or expects me to pay for every single date! But then, there's one. One special piece that maybe, just maybe, fits perfectly. And somehow, you blow it."

Ben whispered from his slumber, "*Just keep swimming.*"

Claire looked at her son. "Did you say something?"

He repeated the words, almost singing. "'*Just keep swimming. Just keep swimming. Just keep swimming, swimming, swimming.*'"

Claire smiled, her heart warmed by Ben's innocent wisdom. She leaned down and kissed him gently on the forehead. "I will, buddy. I will. Goodnight."

~

CLAIRE LEANED against the kitchen sink, her back pressed against the cool metal. She stared at the empty screen on her cell phone, the silence of unanswered texts echoing in her mind. No replies to the several messages she had sent.

"Have you heard from Danny yet?" Nana May asked her tired daughter.

"No. He's pretty upset," she replied. "I did tell him the Andrew living situation was only temporary, but…"

"Why don't you go over and talk to him?" Nana May said softly, trying to help. "You know, honey, sometimes it's not about how much you say, but what you really mean when you do speak."

"I'll just send another text," replied Claire, thinking some dreamy, spiritual lecture from her hippie mom was the last thing she needed right now.

"Why not use a carrier pigeon? It's just as personal, and you won't have to spend a half hour figuring out what cute emojis to add," her mother snapped forcefully. "Now, come and sit. I said, sit!"

For the first time, all three dogs listened to her and sat. So did Claire. Exhausted and overwhelmed, she sank into a chair at the kitchen table. Nana May sat across from her daughter, her eyes filled with a mix of concern and love.

"This generation, always glued to your phones," Nana May said, reaching for Claire's cell to make her point. "This same technology that connects us also keeps us distant from the people right in front of us." She held Claire's gaze intently. "Pause. Take a breath. Take a moment to become more aware, more conscious, and really reflect on the consequences —the implications—of a misplaced word or an unnecessary argument. If we just learn to speak to someone slightly differently, in a different tone, with a different empathy, a different perspective, we would all really connect with people on a different level."

Claire pondered her words for a moment. "That's pretty insightful, Mom. Joni Mitchell?"

"Nah," Nana May chuckled sheepishly. "Jay Shetty. I saw him on YouTube."

They burst into laughter at the irony of it all.

MEDFIELD

Saturday night in Medfield—or as the kids call it, "Deadfield." A super boring town where nothing happened unless you made something happen, like sneaking into someone's house while their parents were out. Plastic 3's parents were away at their new vacation home on Cape Cod, so her place was the go-to for the party. Kids surrounded the keg that her older brother had delivered in his Toyota 4Runner. With Red Solo cups in hand, the teenagers played drinking games in the living room, their carefree laughter and shouts of victory echoing through the house and off the pine trees in the yard.

Skype strolled into the party, trying to keep his excitement in check and play it cool. The room was packed with people talking, laughing, and drinking. This was it—his first real high school house party, and the energy was even more buzzing than he'd imagined. His face lit up when he saw Andrew standing by the keg. He made his way over, weaving through the laughing groups and bobbing heads.

"Yo, Wingman! I thought you were in the city. How'd you get back here?"

Andrew ignored him and downed a Red Solo cup full of beer.

"What are you mad at me for?" Skype asked, confused by the sudden shift in his friend's demeanor.

"You could've just told me you didn't want me around," Andrew snapped, pouring himself another beer from the tap.

"I didn't know anything about—" Skype began, but Andrew wasn't listening. He downed another beer.

Plastic 1 yelled to the crowd, her voice ringing out like a queen's royal decree: "Andrew, tell these guys what you said to Mr. Gleason!"

The room fell silent as all eyes turned his way, eager for the story behind the buzz.

"It was so awesome," giggled Plastic 2.

Andrew, reveling in the celebrity, repeated one of the lines he used to crush Gleason.

"*You are a sad, strange little man, and you have my pity.*"

Someone shouted, "*Yeah! Buzz Lightyear, dude! 'To infinity and beyond!*'" then handed Andrew a full cup from the keg.

The whole party started to chant, "Buzz! Buzz! Buzz! Buzz!" urging Andrew on. He downed the beer, slammed the cup to the ground, and screamed, *"'Aaaarrrrrggghh! Kelly Clarkson!'"*

The crowd erupted in cheers. Skype grew concerned. He leaned to his friend and whispered, "Whoa. Take it easy, Andrew."

With his eyes getting blurry, Andrew looked at Skype and slurred, *"'Grab a drink, don't cost nothin'.'"*

Skype tried to intervene. "Dude, stop. You're drunk."

But Andrew wasn't listening. He draped a condescending arm around Skype's neck and said, *"'Bring me a pitcher of beer every seven minutes until somebody passes out. Then bring one every ten minutes.'"*

He turned to the crowd and shouted, *"We're goin' streakin' in the quad!"*

The place erupted. *"Yeah!! Woo-hoo!"*

Andrew jumped onto a chair, raised his arms to the sky, and screamed, *"'I am a Golden God!'"*

The whole party erupted in cheers. It was official—Andrew was the coolest kid at the party. Maybe the coolest kid in all of Medfield and the surrounding Tri-County area.

Ricky Sherman and his crew showed up at the party fashionably late. No one worth their salt arrives early; it's all about making a cool entrance. As one of the Sidekicks fetched Ricky a beer, he wandered through the house, taking in the scene. He stumbled into a side room that belonged to Plastic 3's older brother—it was a makeshift music studio. Guitars and amps cluttered the space, and posters of famous musicians plastered the walls. Ricky's eyes went wide with envy. So this is what it's like to have supportive parents—parents who encourage your dreams instead of pushing you into sports you don't care about.

He walked through the room, his fingers grazing the strings of a guitar, feeling the smooth wood and imagining the sound. He imagined himself performing in front of an audience. The crowd cheered his name for playing music instead of tackling a quarterback. But the chants from the other room —*"Buzz! Buzz! Buzz!"*—broke his daydream. He set the guitar back on its stand and made his way out.

That's when he saw Andrew, standing on a chair with a wild grin, declaring, *"I am a Golden God!"* Ricky's eyes shot daggers in Andrew's direction, his face darkening with anger.

As Skype meandered through the throng of people surrounding Andrew, his concern grew. He pulled out his cell phone, fingers flying across the screen as he started to text someone. Suddenly, he collided with Ricky, who was fuming with barely contained rage.

"What are you doing here, Freak?" Ricky sneered, shoving Skype hard against the wall. The thud echoed through the room, grabbing a few curious glances from partygoers, but most were too caught up in the festivities to pay much attention.

Skype grimaced but quickly managed to send his text before slipping away.

PETERSON HOUSE

Saturday night in *"Deadfield,"* and Molly was home alone reading a book, as usual. She used to have friends—a lot of friends, actually—back in grade school. They would sit and talk and laugh and comb each other's hair and have playdates and dance parties. Then the internet came along, and suddenly all her friends were in chat rooms with AIM screen names, talking about boy bands and the latest TV reality shows like *American Idol, Survivor,* and *The Bachelor.* They didn't sit and talk anymore; they just sent each other messages.

That was around the same time Ben started having problems. He couldn't stand any kind of light or noise, so Molly and Claire started to speak in hushed tones and turned off anything electronic. They never made a conscious decision to get rid of computers and TV; they just stopped using them.

Eventually, the television in the living room became just another piece of furniture. When Claire moved the family from Baltimore to Medfield, taking the TV along wasn't even an option. Over time, not having a television in the house became the new normal—whatever "normal" means.

At first, Molly resented her brother for making them go without electronics. She was especially jealous of all the attention he received from their mother. Eventually, Molly found her escape in books, and over time, she built a hard exterior to shelter herself from the outside world. They could keep their pop culture, social media, and Instagram influencers. Fiercely independent, Molly forced herself to avoid their reality TV shows and immature internet videos. She wore it like a badge of honor. She was not about to become just another cookie-cutter Plastic.

Maybe high school would be different, she thought—a fresh start. Perhaps all those grade school friends who used to sit and talk with her would do so again. Maybe if her mother let her have a TV, she could sit at the cool cafeteria table near the bathrooms and talk about the latest shows. But high school wasn't different. It was just more of the same. And Molly decided that she liked being different. Well, sometimes. Sometimes, she thought, it might be nice to have a TV and be part of the conversation. But she would never admit that—especially to the *Plastics*.

Underneath it all, Molly missed being "normal"—whatever that means. But most of all, she missed her best friend, Jenna.

Jenna and Molly were pretty much their own little group since fifth grade, somewhere between super popular and, well, not. Not brainy, not jocks, not rich, not druggies, not mean, not goody-goody. They both didn't know if the two of them found each other because they were alike in so many ways, or if, because they found each other, they became so alike in so many ways. Molly remembered how they both screamed with delight the day they found out they were going to be in the same homeroom. That's why Molly couldn't understand what was going on with them lately, now that they were actually in high school. It was nothing like she thought it would be.

It all happened over the summer.

Jenna's father was a big-time Boston lawyer who won a case or got a huge bonus or hit the lottery or something. All Molly knew was that Jenna left in early June and spent the whole summer on Cape Cod at their new house—which was sure to have a television in every room so Jenna could watch all the latest reality shows. When the family came back just before Labor Day, everything changed. Jenna had attached herself to a new crowd, destined for high school glory.

Molly didn't see Jenna until the first day of school, and she was shocked. Her friend looked so different. Her hair was colored platinum blond, and she was wearing a skirt that seemed way too short for school. It was totally not her style. Jenna had always worn modest clothes and hardly any makeup. They both did. But it wasn't just the way Jenna looked that was different—she was acting differently too. She was nice enough. She'd say hi when she passed Molly in the hallway, but only if she wasn't with the other *Plastics*—and she was rarely without the *Plastics*.

You see, popular girls never go anywhere alone—one of the ironclad rules of popularity is that you always travel in packs. So, by the laws of popularity, the unpopular ones like Molly and Skype are left to navigate high school solo. Molly eventually gave up on the cafeteria altogether, preferring to avoid the fake *"Sorry, there's no room for you at our table"* moments. It was just easier to find refuge in the library, surrounded by books rather than people. Molly had always prided herself on rising above typical, petty teenage drama, but that first week of school, watching Jenna and the *Plastics* at the cool table in the cafeteria, she experienced firsthand what it felt like to be lonely. Really lonely.

~

MOLLY HAD her nose buried in a book, the soft glow of her mother's ancient Dell laptop illuminating the room. The old machine, a relic from another era, struggled with every keystroke—proof that social worker salaries don't stretch to the latest MacBooks. Next to the keyboard was the crumpled piece of paper handed to her by the *Plastics* with the words *"TOP ROMANTIC MOVIE SCENES"* scrawled across it. Molly tapped away at the keyboard, her fingers moving quickly as she typed the phrase into the search bar. With each click of the mouse, Molly's face grew more and more disappointed. The screen filled with lists of romantic scenes from classics like *Sixteen Candles*, *Say Anything*, and *The Notebook*. The realization hit her slowly—the "original" ideas she'd shared with Andrew were nothing more than stolen moments from these movies.

She typed a new search into the bar, trying to find something more unique. As she hit enter, a scene from *The Breakfast Club* began to play. Emilio Estevez turned to Molly Ringwald and delivered the line, *"I mean, we're all pretty bizarre. Some of us are just better at hiding it, that's all."*

She looked as if she were about to cry when her cell phone buzzed.

MEDFIELD MA

Molly carefully navigated her way through the crowded living room, dodging groups of people yelling and laughing loudly. The music pulsed in the background as she weaved between the tightly packed bodies, her eyes scanning the room until they finally landed on Skype. He stood near the edge of the room, looking a little out of place, his gaze fixed on his phone.

"I came as soon as I got your text. What's up with him?"

"I don't know," Skype replied, his voice tinged with nervousness. "He's a mess."

Suddenly, Andrew spotted Molly across the room. With his speech slurred from alcohol, he yelled, "Hey, Molly's here! Look, everybody, it's Molly!"

Molly forced her way through the crowd and grabbed him by the arm. "Andrew, I think it's time to go home."

"Sure," Andrew smiled. "Good idea. Home. I'm off to your house." He took a few steps, then paused. "But wait. It's only temporary, right? Like, a rental?"

Molly sensed something was wrong. Andrew's demeanor shifted, turning bitter as he pulled his arm away from her. "No, wait. I'm not going to your house. You don't even have a TV."

The crowd chuckled. Skype intervened, "Come on, Andrew. Let's go."

Andrew looked up. "Oops, sorry, Molly. Guess I'm going to Skype's house now. His turn to rent me. At least he has a TV. A huge one, too. Only, he doesn't have anybody to watch it with him."

Skype was hurt. He whispered, "Why are you doing this?"

Andrew continued his drunken rant. "Hey, I know! We can go to your house and watch your computer. Show me all your funny little videos. Just me and you, 'cause nobody's ever gonna see them, are they? 'Cause you're too scared."

That cut Skype deep. He looked at Andrew and snapped, "You know what? Screw you!" Then he ran out of the room.

"Go ahead. Go home," Andrew yelled after him, his voice a mix of jealousy, anger, and hurt. "Home to your big TV and your movies... and your perfect family."

Even in his intoxicated state, Andrew realized he had crossed a line, but it was too late. Skype was already gone.

Molly pulled at Andrew's arm, spinning him to look directly into her eyes. "All this time, I thought you were smart and funny and original. Were any of those ideas your own?"

She knew the answer. She just wanted to hear him say it. But Andrew said nothing.

"Turns out you've just been hiding behind movies this whole time. So, who's really the scared one?"

Her words felt like a punch to the gut, and before Andrew could react, Molly was gone, storming out of the party.

Suddenly, the room seemed smaller, the noise fading into the background as he stood there, friendless and more alone than ever.

JOHNSON HOUSE

Skype stormed into his Man Cave, his eyes bloodshot from crying. He ripped open the closet door, grabbed handfuls of VHS tapes and DVDs, and hurled them across the room. The tapes clattered against the walls, their cases cracking, but he didn't care. His legs buckled, and he sank, defeated, into the beanbag chair, a heartbroken sound tearing from his throat as fresh tears streamed down his face.

The doorbell sliced through the quiet downstairs. Muffled voices and the heavy tread of footsteps followed, growing louder until they stopped right outside his door. It swung open, and there stood Mrs. Johnson, looking all worried, and Officer Muldoon, doing his usual serious-cop thing. There was someone else lurking behind them, a blurry shape, but Skype was too upset to even bother looking. He just didn't care who it was.

"Michael," Mrs. Johnson said. "Do you know where Andrew is?"

"Well, he's not here!" Skype snapped, trying to mask his hurt and anger.

"Watch your tone, young man," his mother scolded.

Skype sat up and collected himself, wiping his nose with his sleeve.

"Sorry. What… what's this all about?" he asked, his eyes shifting to the mysterious person lingering in the doorway.

Muldoon stepped aside, revealing a woman in her forties. She was tall, with kind eyes that seemed to take everything in, and her dark hair was pulled back in a tight, no-nonsense ponytail. She wore a simple dark jacket, and though her expression was serious, there was a gentle strength about her.

"Skype," he said solemnly. "This is Allison Wilden. Andrew's mother."

MEDFIELD

Andrew stumbled down Main Street, his mind foggy as he passed the usual spots—the local diner, the convenience store, the Dunkin' Donuts, the pizza place. Light snowflakes started to fall, swirling in the air before melting as soon as they hit the ground.

He stopped in front of the vacant, shingled video store that was once his home, his world. The windows were dark, the door shut tight. Andrew reached into his pocket and pulled out the black remote control, his thumb hovering over the buttons. He pointed it at the window, half-hoping, half-dreaming that maybe—just maybe—he could rewind everything back to the way it was.

CLICK. CLICK. CLICK.

Nothing.

The remote was just a piece of plastic, and the store stayed empty—a silent reminder of everything that had changed. Of course, it didn't work. Nothing worked anymore. It used to, before. Before his mom left. Before his dad's breakdown. Before he felt like he was nothing more than everybody else's problem.

CRASH!

He hurled the remote through the *COMING ATTRACTIONS* sign stenciled on the front bay window, glass shattering in a burst of anger and frustration.

Suddenly, there was a screech of tires behind him. Before he could react, arms grabbed him, shoving him into the backseat of a car. The door slammed shut, and the car roared into gear, speeding off into the night.

KING PHILIP OVERLOOK

Ricky and the Sidekicks surrounded Andrew against the railing overlooking Medfield. It was the same spot he had shared with Molly; only this time he wasn't *"King of the World"* Jack Dawson—he was just drunk, sad, angry Andrew Wilden.

The snow was falling harder now, spinning and twirling under the moonlight. Andrew sized up the situation and addressed the threatening clan.

"The first rule of Fight Club is: You do not talk about Fight Club."

"What's this kid's deal?" Ricky demanded, his fists clenched so tightly his knuckles turned white.

Andrew locked eyes with him, his expression dark and unyielding, like a coiled snake ready to strike.

"Say 'what' again. I dare you. I double dare you."

Stretching his body, arms raised high, one leg poised in the Karate Kid crane stance, Andrew said, *"If done right... can no defense."*

Ricky looked to the Sidekicks. "What the hell is he doing?"

"It's just lines from movies, dude," replied a Sidekick. "That's all he ever does."

Drunk Andrew leaned forward and whispered to the menacing crew, *"There are a lot of things about me you don't know anything about. Things you wouldn't understand. Things you couldn't understand. Things you shouldn't understand."*

Ricky stepped closer, his voice oozing angry confidence. "Oh, but I do know. I saw your file. Never went to school, never even left that shitty, run-down video store. I've got it all figured out. Or maybe I should just quote a movie," he said, adopting a mocking high-pitched tone. *"Mother? Mother, where are you?"*

One of the Sidekicks leaned in and whispered, "Is that from *Bambi*? Wow, that's harsh, man."

"And your old man?" Ricky snarled, almost nose to nose with Andrew. "He's completely nuts."

Andrew clenched his fist and swung, but the punch missed

wildly. The Sidekicks grabbed his arms, holding him firmly. Andrew struggled to break free, but it was no use.

"You think you can come to my school and be the… what did you call it? *Golden God?* That ain't how the pecking order works," Ricky taunted, grabbing Andrew tight by the collar.

"*Two hits. Me hitting you, you hitting the floor.*"

As Ricky cocked his arm back, ready to strike, Andrew gazed up at the snowy Medfield sky with a distant, thousand-yard stare.

"*Toto—I've got a feeling we're not in Kansas anymore,*" he muttered softly.

Then, everything went black.

PETERSON HOUSE

Claire sat curled up on the couch, her book resting on her lap as she flipped through its pages absentmindedly. She glanced up when Molly walked through the front door.

"Another adventurous date with Andrew?" she asked.

"I don't think we'll be going on any more adventures for a while," Molly replied sadly, then snuggled her head onto her mother's shoulder. Claire watched her daughter, who looked completely drained. It had clearly been a rough day for her too. Claire, for her part, just tried to savor the quiet moment before whatever was coming next.

"You used to fit right in here, curled up in the triangle of my leg. Remember? This is nice, *right? Right?*"

"I remember," Molly said softly, longing for those simpler times. Sometimes she just wanted to curl up into a tiny little ball and let her mother hug her and kiss her all over. She missed being a kid—back when life was just about scraped knees and endless summer days, free from the exhausting tightrope walk of social clichés and peer pres-sure, Instagram, Facebook, and how many *likes* you had. She yearned for the days before she worried about saying the "right" thing, wearing the "right" clothes, or being seen with the "right" crowd. Simpler times, before every move felt judged and fitting in seemed more important than just being.

"You'll be off to college soon."

"In a few years, Mom."

"I know, but still," Claire said, reflecting for a moment and realizing that raising children is really just a series of goodbyes.

"Were you popular in high school?" Molly asked.

Claire stroked her daughter's hair and smiled. "I was cuspy."

"Cuspy? What's that mean?"

"I was always on the edges, you know? I'd flit in and out of groups. I never thought anyone should be labeled, so I was friends with everyone."

They sat for a while, enjoying the quiet.

"Sounds nice," Molly said. "Kids can be really mean."

"Kids are mean because they're honest and don't know any better. But mostly, I think it's just because they're really stupid," Claire said with a laugh.

That made Molly smile. She nestled her head deeper into her mother's shoulder and sighed, "Why are boys so complicated?"

Claire paused and continued to stroke her daughter's hair, thinking about what to say, unsure how to answer because she didn't have a simple solution.

"I don't know, sweetie," she sighed back. "I hate to tell you, but it doesn't get any easier when they become men."

"Everything he's been telling me is a lie," Molly admitted, her voice heavy with disappointment.

"Sometimes it's easier to be someone else than to let the world see who you really are. Being yourself can be really scary." Claire thought for a moment, then looked directly at her daughter—not lecturing, but speaking from the heart. "We all hide because we're afraid. Afraid of being seen for who we really are, flaws and all. But the bravest thing you can ever do, the absolute bravest, is let your true self shine, even when it feels like the hardest thing in the world."

Molly slumped back into the couch, wiping away a tear. Claire could see her daughter was hurting, and though she didn't have all the answers, she tried to offer comfort. "Andrew has been really good to your brother," she mentioned softly.

Molly absorbed the words in silence as Claire glanced around the living room.

"You think maybe we should get a TV?"

Molly cherished the quiet moment with her mom. "Nah, I think we'll be fine without one."

"I think we'll be fine too," Claire agreed, kissing her daughter tenderly on the forehead. Molly hugged her tightly.

"Goodnight, Mom."

"Goodnight, sweetheart," Claire replied, smiling proudly as she watched her mature, fiercely independent, and now heartbroken teenage daughter head upstairs.

Suddenly, Claire's cell phone buzzed.

DANNY MULDOON.

"Danny? Listen, I am so sorry..." Her face fell as she listened. "What? I thought he was at Mrs. O'Hara's?... I'll be right there."

She grabbed her car keys and rushed out the door.

JOHNSON HOUSE

Andrew woke up, his vision blurred and his head pounding. He blinked through the groggy haze, trying to make sense of his surroundings. The room was cluttered with DVD cases and VHS cassettes, stacked on shelves and scattered across the floor. For a moment, he could have sworn he was back home.

Maybe this was all just a dream.

Yeah, that's it. Like those flashbacks and dream sequences in movies.

He rubbed his eyes as a woman gently wiped his forehead

with a cool, damp cloth. In his foggy state, Andrew whispered, "Mom?"

Slowly, Andrew's surroundings came into focus. He wasn't back home at his video store on Main Street. Instead, he was in Skype's Man Cave, surrounded by movie posters and stacks of DVDs. Mrs. Johnson was sitting beside him, her face full of concern. As he blinked away the grogginess, he tried to remember how he'd ended up here, feeling the weight of everything that had happened.

"Sorry," Andrew murmured. "I... I thought you were someone else."

Mrs. Johnson gave him a caring, reassuring smile and tenderly touched his face.

"Everything is going to be OK, honey. I'll get you more ice."

As Mrs. Johnson left the room, a figure emerged in the doorway. Andrew couldn't quite make out who it was at first. The figure approached slowly, tentatively, until finally, there she stood—his mother, Allison Wilden. She paused, her hands wringing together nervously, not sure what to do.

"I heard about your father. I came as soon as I..." Allison began, her voice shaky.

"Really?" Andrew interrupted sharply, not letting her finish and looking away. "The police said they left you a bunch of messages."

He could feel the anger boiling up inside him, mixing with the confusion and hurt. The sight of his mother standing there, after so much time and so many unanswered questions, felt overwhelming.

Allison took a hesitant step closer, her eyes pleading. "Andrew, I... I didn't know how to..."

But Andrew cut her off again, his voice rising. "Didn't know how to what? Didn't know how to answer your phone?"

The words hung in the air. Allison's face crumpled, and she took a step back, her eyes beginning to glisten. Andrew's heart pounded in his chest. He didn't know if he could ever forgive her—or if he even wanted to try.

Allison tried to explain, "I was away and…."

"Away," Andrew snapped, the bitterness palpable. "Must be nice."

"We were filming and…" she tried to continue, but Andrew wasn't listening. He turned his head away, staring at the cluttered shelves filled with DVDs and VHS tapes.

Allison glanced down at the floor, gathering her thoughts. "I wanted to come see you so many times, Andrew. I would sit at the train station for hours, trying to decide, but…" She trailed off, knowing there was no excuse that could ever justify her absence.

"Your father," she continued, her voice softer, "he has a big heart, but he's… different. You understand that now. I'm glad he's getting help. You two were so close. You had your movies, your banter. Sometimes… well, sometimes I felt like I didn't fit in, you know?"

Andrew could sense his mother's pain. Finally, he looked up and studied the woman in front of him. His mother had aged a bit since the last time he saw her. She looked softer, more composed, but there was something else about her; Andrew could see it in her eyes and in the way she carried herself.

As Allison sat down gingerly on the edge of the bed, Andrew noticed a change in her. His mother seemed different now—content, as if she had finally found comfort in her own skin. She belonged to something.

Allison looked at her son, her expression a mix of remorse and longing. "I know it was wrong, leaving. I told myself it was a lesson. That if I could walk out, you'd know you could too. That you wouldn't get stuck in someone else's story,"

They both sat in silence for a moment, Allison hoping her words were getting through. "Do you remember what I used to whisper in your ear?"

"Every day," Andrew replied quietly, simply. *Life isn't like in the movies. You need to write your own ending."*

He touched his swollen black eye and said, "I'm kinda finding that out."

Allison gazed at her teenage son with pride, seeing how grown, how handsome, how mature he had become. "I hoped someday you would understand," she said softly.

They both sensed that there was so much more to say, so many emotions pent up inside both of them, but they held them back—choosing silence instead, giving them a sense of understanding and a chance for a new beginning.

"Do you know why your father and I named the store *Coming Attractions*?" Allison asked, her voice soft with nostalgia. "*Coming Attractions* meant all the great things ahead of you. We wanted you to believe there was always something ahead. Something magical. Even when real life wasn't." She paused, then softly admitted, "Even when we weren't."

Andrew smiled. He had spent so much time being angry, feeling abandoned, that he hadn't allowed himself to see his mother's pain, her struggles. He looked at his mother—really looked at her—and saw the love and regret etched in her face.

"It's okay, Mom," he reassured her with a smile. "I'm fine."

She nodded, cupping his face gently in her hands, her eyes glistening. "I know. I missed you so much," she admitted softly.

"I missed you too," he replied.

Mrs. Johnson returned to the room with an ice pack for Andrew's eye and gently placed it against his swelling bruise. It was the kind of caring Allison Wilden had neglected to give her own son, and she suddenly felt out of place.

"I should go," Allison admitted softly.

Andrew watched his mother stand and turn to leave, but this time he called out, "Mom?"

Allison stopped in her tracks.

"I hear NYU has a really good film school," Andrew said. "Maybe I can come check it out."

A smile spread across her face. "I'd love that," she replied.

That was it. Those three simple words gave Andrew something a hundred apologies or rehearsed explanations couldn't. Allison wrapped her arms around her son and kissed him on the forehead and on the face like she was breathing him in, reassuring him that everything was going to be alright.

Skype peeked his head in from behind the door as Mrs. Johnson escorted Allison Wilden out.

"Hey," he said meekly.

"Hey."

"So, my mom made this for you," Skype said, handing Andrew a plate of dry white toast. Andrew smiled at the *Blues Brothers* joke between them.

"I was a real jerk last night," Andrew admitted.

"Yep. You sure were," Skype agreed, nodding. He waited for a moment before continuing, "You were right, though. I should put myself out there. So, you moving to New York now?"

"I don't know. Got school on Monday," Andrew replied with a sad, forced cheer. "*Go Pirates. Aargh.*"

"Well, make sure someone shows you around. Like, where the cool kids sit and stuff. You're gonna want the right crew, ya know?" Skype suggested, doing his best to mask his sadness. "At least you won't have to deal with Ricky and the Dumb Dumbs anymore."

They sat in silence, feeling the weight of uncertainty. Andrew propped himself up on the bed.

"So, wingman, let me ask you a question," he said thoughtfully as he surveyed the Man Cave filled with VHS tapes, DVDs, audio/video equipment, and cameras. "You know how to work any of this stuff?"

The friends looked at each other, and their eyes suddenly widened as an idea formed—and they began to hatch a plan.

MEDFIELD HIGH SCHOOL

Monday morning at Medfield High. Students shuffled through the halls, heads down, earplugs firmly in place, no one paying attention to anything but their own digital world. The flat-screen television monitors mounted along the corridors mechanically scrolled through the morning announcements, but no one paid them any mind. As usual, students were too focused on texting friends, liking Facebook posts, and posting Instagram stories.

Suddenly, a piercing screech of microphone feedback echoed through the school's PA system, shattering the monotony. Everyone stopped in their tracks. Students exchanged glances. The interruption had achieved what seemed impossible—bringing the bustling halls of Medfield High to a complete standstill and making everyone finally look up from their phones.

A voice boomed over the loudspeakers.

"Gooooood Mooooorning Red Raiders!"

The TV monitors lining the hallways flickered and scrambled, casting an eerie glow as the haunting theme from *The Twilight Zone* began to play. And then, as if stepping out of another dimension, a black-and-white vision of Skype appeared on the screens. He was transformed into a modern-day Rod Serling—his hair slicked back with Brylcreem and dressed impeccably in a dark suit with a thin black tie. Skype spoke directly into the camera. His voice, full of deep dramatic flair, echoed through the hallways.

"Submitted for your approval. I give you the High School Athlete."

An image of Ricky Sherman appeared on every screen.

"He's popular. Admired. Feared. But he peaks at sixteen," Skype announced. "Suddenly, he blows out a knee. It's rehab. Low SAT scores. Then it's off to Community College. Before you know it, he's living in Mom's basement with a comb-over, a dad bod, and he's mowing our lawns."

A photoshopped depiction of a sad-looking, middle-aged Ricky Sherman filled the screens. He had a beer belly, an exaggerated wispy comb-over, and wore a bright orange landscaper jumpsuit. Students burst into laughter, watching the goofy transformation of the once-feared jock.

Then, Ricky's voice rang through the halls via the PA system, cutting through the laughter.

"See, I got a system here—a pecking order, if you will," Ricky declared, his tone as confident and unapologetic as the day he delivered it to Andrew in the cafeteria. "*The Nerds* do the work for me, and I let them survive high school. Fair trade if you ask me."

Skype's voice resonated through the speakers.

"It all started in 7th grade..."

On the TV monitors, a grainy video clip flickered to life. It showed a younger Ricky Sherman, his middle school hair spiked with an outrageous amount of gel, hunched over his desk. His eyes darted around nervously as he copied answers from a classmate's paper, leaning in so close his face nearly touched the desk. The camera, set up by Skype while he was home sick that year, captured every sneaky, dishonest, bully move Ricky made.

Skype continued speaking as Rod Serling.

"...and it hasn't changed much today."

The screens flickered and switched to a series of more recent clips, all captured on Skype's cell phone. Each video showed Ricky Sherman's bullying antics: one clip captured him punching a Geek in the hallway, another showed him holding a Nerd in a headlock, and yet another had him shoving students aside like they were in his way. The final clip was the kicker—Ricky sneaking into Mr. Gleason's classroom to snap photos of a midterm exam. It was clear that Skype's knack for filming every moment in Medfield High was finally paying off.

His voice echoed with determination over the PA system.

"How many times have we been taken advantage of?

Made to sit in the front of the classroom and the back of the cafeteria?!"

Everyone was riveted by Skype's impassioned speech. In the cafeteria, the Geeky Nerd with the long bangs sat at the back table, his eyes wide with awe as he absorbed every word. Mr. Costello, the underappreciated janitor, stood in the hallway, leaning on his broom and nodding along with a look of quiet approval. Even Mrs. Scully, the overworked receptionist, paused mid-task, her fingers frozen over the keyboard as she stopped what she was doing to listen.

On the TV monitors, Skype's image had transformed into the President of the United States. He was wearing a sharp suit and red tie, standing at a podium as if he were addressing the nation.

"We are fighting for our right to live. To exist. We will not go quietly into the night! We will not vanish without a fight! We're going to live on! We're going to survive! Today we celebrate our Independence Day!"

Applause erupted throughout the school halls. In rapid succession, the TV screens flashed scenes from movies, each clip showcasing a moment where bullies met their match.

- Ralphie from *A Christmas Story* delivering a decisive beating to Scut Farkus.
- The carload of O'Doyle boys plummeting off a cliff in *Billy Madison*.
- Johnny Lawrence getting a well-deserved kick in the face from Daniel in *The Karate Kid*.
- Regina George being hit by a bus in *Mean Girls*.
- Marty McFly landing a knockout punch on Biff Tannen in *Back to the Future*.

Skype appeared on screen once more, this time decked out as the fierce warrior from *Braveheart*. His hair was wild and unkempt, and his face was painted a vibrant blue. With a butchered Scottish accent, he roared his message with dramatic flair:

"Would you be willin' to trade ALL the days for one chance, just one chance, to tell our enemies that they may take our homework... but they'll never take... OUR FREEDOM!"

Cheers erupted throughout the halls, spilling into the parking lot and the courtyard. The whole school was buzzing with excitement!

Finally, Skype appeared on screen again, but this time as himself. His expression was serious and resolute as he looked directly into the camera, speaking with determined intensity as if he were addressing every student in Medfield, every town, the whole state, the whole nation, and the world beyond.

"The question isn't who is going to let me; it's who is going to stop me."

His words, echoing Ayn Rand's defiant declaration—the same one from his mother's yellow sticky note—sparked a wave of rebellion and empowerment throughout the school.

In the cafeteria, the Geeky Nerd stood up and poured milk over a Jock, flashing a triumphant grin as he brushed his bangs out of his eyes. SLAM! An overweight girl, fueled by newfound courage, body-slammed Plastic 1 into their locker with a powerful shove. Mrs. Scully flung folders into the trash with gusto. Mr. Costello, the underappreciated janitor, let his mop drop beside a rancid spill of lunch food, his face breaking into a wide, liberating smile.

Meanwhile, Ricky Sherman was in full-on panic mode. He sprinted through the halls, desperately trying to shut off the television monitors blaring his embarrassing moments and bullying tactics. He leaped to reach one of the screens but missed, crashing into Principal Shepherd instead. Ricky was totally busted.

CORRIGAN MENTAL HEALTH CENTER

Claire and Andrew walked down the sterile, clinical hallway of the Corrigan Mental Health Center, the sound of his sneakers squeaking against the polished floor. The place smelled like a hospital, with a clinical, antiseptic scent that permeated every corner.

"So, um, how's Molly?" Andrew asked, a bit of hesitation in his voice.

"She'll come around," Claire assured him. "Just give her time."

They stopped at a closed door. Claire draped an arm around Andrew's shoulders; her touch was gentle yet firm, a silent gesture of support.

"Everybody needs time to settle in and adjust," she added gently. "The nurses said he's doing better. Might even be out sooner than we thought."

Andrew hesitated, but Claire nodded encouragingly, signaling for him to go in alone. After gathering his courage, he stepped inside, uncertain of what awaited him.

At the far end of the room, James Wilden sat in a chair by the window, looking overwhelmed and distant. Andrew approached slowly.

"Hey, Dad," he whispered tentatively. "How... how you doin'?"

Mr. Wilden's expression flickered with a mixture of joy and embarrassment upon seeing his son. His eyes briefly sparkled with happiness, but it was soon clouded by a profound sadness. He shifted uneasily in his chair.

"I'm sorry I haven't come by. I wanted to, but they said you needed some time…" Andrew said.

His father interrupted, gently reaching out and touching the bruise on his son's face.

"Your eye."

"I'm fine," Andrew reassured him. "Just some kids at school."

Mr. Wilden raised an eyebrow. "School?" Then, after a moment, he said with a soft, reassuring smile, "That's good."

The squeak of shoes echoed down the hallway as a nurse approached. She had a gentle expression and muscular arms, and Andrew noticed a tattoo on the inside of her forearm: *Slow down, you crazy child,* written in flowing cursive. It was a line from a Billy Joel song, and Andrew wondered if she quoted songs the way he quoted movies. It seemed like everyone had something they used as a shield.

"How are we doing today, Mr. Wilden?" she asked. "This must be your son. So handsome."

Andrew looked around the room. "Could you bring my dad a television? He likes to watch movies."

"We thought it was best to keep him busy with other activities," the nurse told Andrew. "Your father has a very full schedule."

"Oh. OK," Andrew replied, then turned to his father. "Dad, I need to tell you something. I, um. I saw mo..."

What Andrew wanted to say was, *Mom. I saw Mom! She's back, here in Medfield, and we're all going to move home to the video store and live happily ever after, just like in the movies.* But he knew that wasn't the truth. He also knew that it was OK. It was all going to be OK.

Instead, he said, "Movie. I saw a movie. It's about a kid who goes to high school. He's the new kid, kind of a fish out of water, and..."

Suddenly, the DING of a text message interrupted his story. The nurse reached into her smock for her cell phone and apologized. "I'm sorry. I should have put that on mute."

James Wilden looked at his son knowingly and gave a familiar wink. *"Get her. She's givin' out wings."*

The nurse looked up from her phone. "Is that from *It's a Wonderful Life*? That's my favorite movie. Have you ever seen it?"

Mr. Wilden said, "Bing!"

Andrew smiled wide, and his father beamed, super proud.

"Now, son. You were telling me about this high school movie?" urged Mr. Wilden.

"Yeah. Yeah. This kid has to go to a new school. He's the outcast, right? So, he needs to make new friends and..."

Andrew's brown eyes sparkled as he told his story, and Mr. Wilden's face beamed with pride, hanging on his son's every word.

BOSTON CITY HIGH SCHOOL

Andrew walked the halls of his new school, immediately struck by how different it was from Medfield High. The atmosphere was edgier, more urban, with hallways that seemed to pulse with a restless energy. The walls were covered in graffiti, the lockers dented and worn, and the students rushed past, absorbed in their digital worlds. Everyone was lost in their screens, thumbs tapping away on Instagram, Facebook, Snapchat—completely oblivious to their surroundings and each other. Nobody took a second look. Nobody noticed him. Nobody knew who he was. Some things never change.

Andrew found himself alone at his locker, struggling with the stubborn combination lock.

"*Perfect,*" he muttered under his breath. "*Here we go again.*"

Suddenly, a student rushed by, shouting to a group of kids gathered by the vending machines. "Guys! Did you hear what happened over at Medfield High? Check this out."

The crowd quickly gathered around the screen of his phone. A YouTube video played, and Andrew could hear Skype's voice echoing through the hallway: "*The question isn't who is going to let me; it's who is going to stop me.*"

Laughter and cheers erupted as the students watched the video of Skype's spirited speech.

"This kid's got a hundred thousand likes already!" someone exclaimed, their voice filled with awe and admiration.

Andrew couldn't help but feel a surge of pride for Skype.

His best friend.

The internet sensation.

O'HARA HOUSE

Andrew plopped his backpack on the couch, feeling exhausted and deflated after his first day at the new school. *Go Pirates.* More like *Ugh!* than *Aaargh!*

The doorbell rang, breaking the quiet of the house. Andrew hesitated for a moment before getting up to answer it. Standing on Mrs. O'Hara's front porch was Molly, holding cue cards in her hand. She put a finger to her lips, signaling for Andrew to be quiet, and then began dropping the cards in succession onto the porch floor. Andrew watched in amusement as Molly acted out the scene from *Love Actually.*

...SOMETIMES...

...IT'S EASIER...

...TO BE OTHER PEOPLE....

A card showed pictures of Leonardo DiCaprio, Matthew Broderick, Emilio Estevez, and Judd Nelson—all actors from the movies Andrew had quoted.

Molly continued to flip the cards.

...BUT, FOR FEAR OF COPYRIGHT ISSUES...

...AND BECAUSE I STILL DON'T OWN A TELEVISION...

...LET ME SAY...

...IN MY OWN WORDS...

...I LOVE YOU...

...ACTUALLY.

Andrew's eyes lit up. "You saw that movie?!"

"Skype showed me," Molly replied. "Have you seen it?"

Andrew gave her a look that said, *you're kidding, right?*

"Wait," Andrew exclaimed. "I got you something." He rushed off to the other room and returned, hiding something behind his back. With a mischievous grin, he extended his hand, revealing a small Emperor Penguin stuffed animal.

"You're my heartsong," he said. Then Andrew pulled Molly in close and wrapped an arm around her waist. "I owe you an apology. For everything that happened. I really wasn't myself."

Molly's cheeks turned a shade of pink, and her eyes glistened with happiness as she met his gaze. "Well, I think I like *this* Andrew a whole lot better than *Movie-Guy* Andrew."

MEDFIELD HIGH SCHOOL

The gym had undergone a magical transformation into a prom night straight out of the 1980s. The whole place was a neon-colored, retro paradise. Music blared from the speakers, playing Duran Duran, Phil Collins, Wham!, and Michael Jackson songs. Girls with oversized neon earrings and side ponytails danced with boys sporting stone-washed jeans and bomber jackets to the thumping bass line of *Billie Jean*. Posters of '80s movie icons adorned the walls: the cast of *The Breakfast Club*, Michael J. Fox next to the DeLorean in *Back to the Future*, and Tom Cruise wearing his Ray-Ban sunglasses in *Risky Business*.

The *Plastics*, dressed as Madonna, Cyndi Lauper, and Pat Benatar, rushed over to Molly and Andrew, their excitement infectious.

"This '80s theme was such a brilliant idea!" Plastic 1 (Madonna) exclaimed, the others nodding in agreement. "We kept it authentic, so no cell phones, no texting, no social media. Honestly, it feels kinda free to be disconnected for a while," she added with a smile.

She turned to Andrew. "So, how's everything going at the new school? Surviving the Pirates?"

Andrew grinned. "*Barely*, but I'm getting the hang of it."

"And how's your dad doing?" Plastic 2 (Cyndi Lauper) asked, genuinely meaning it. "We heard he's getting better."

Andrew's smile widened. "Yeah, he's better."

Plastic 3 (Pat Benatar) finally spoke up and looked at Molly.

"I heard Ben is doing better too. That's great."

Molly looked at her, a bit surprised she would ask.

"He's good. Thanks for asking, Jenna."

"Don't you mean Plastic number 3?" Jenna replied, smiling her old best-friend-from-middle-school smile at Molly.

Molly smiled back, and they hugged—and for the very first time in a very long time, Molly felt absolutely happy.

The music got louder, and the dance floor filled with students doing the moonwalk, the running man, and the Kid 'N Play moves. Then, all eyes turned as Skype made his grand entrance. Dressed like Duckie from *Pretty in Pink*—round glasses, bolo tie, hip fedora hat, and white pointy-toed shoes—he was chock-full of confidence. On his arm was a stunning tall beauty—his Instagram model girlfriend. Envy rippled through the crowd, and Skype soaked in the attention with an enormous shit-eatin' grin that spread from ear to ear. People ran over to give him high-fives and daps.

"Gnarly, dude."

"Righteous."

Even Plastic 1 gave him a stamp of approval. *"Rad. Like, total-Ē Rad."*

Andrew pulled Molly aside, wrapping his arm around her. They began to slow dance, moving as if they were the only two people in the gym, in the school, in the entire world. Inch by inch, their bodies drew closer as the music reverberated off the high ceiling and concrete walls.

Andrew looked into her eyes, a tender smile spreading across his face. "My dad always said this about movies: 'You don't truly see something until the second time. You need to know the ending to really get how perfectly it all fit together from the start.'" He paused, that happy, warm smile growing. "But not you," he added softly. *"I thought you were perfect the very first time I saw you."*

Their breath quickened with every movement, hearts pounding, until finally, gently and tenderly, Andrew leaned in and kissed Molly. It was magic. Better than any kiss Andrew had ever seen in the movies.

Better than when Sam kissed Molly in *Ghost.*

Better than Westley kissing Buttercup in *The Princess Bride.*

Better than Noah and Allie's crazy kiss in the rain from *The Notebook.*

Even better than the upside-down kiss between Mary Jane Watson and Peter Parker in *Spider-Man.*

It was a kiss full of magic and yearning and wonder and hope.

CHILD PROTECTIVE SERVICES OFFICE

Claire stared at her messy office, determination in her thoughts. *This is it. Today is the day. Today is the day I start to arrange things. Organize things. Toss things out. Get my life together.* She leaned back, scanned the disheveled room one more time, and sighed.

"Maybe tomorrow."

Gazing out the window, she noticed a police car parked outside the building. Her heart skipped a beat, hoping it was Danny Muldoon.

As Officer Kobolowski approached her office, her excitement faded.

"Miss Peterson?" he addressed her.

Claire did her best to hide her disappointment.

"Yes? Oh my God, what's wrong? Is it Ben? My mother?" Her anxiety spilled out in rapid-fire questions.

"No, no. Everyone is fine," Kobolowski reassured her quickly. "I promise. But you'll need to come with me."

"Why?" Claire asked, suspicion creeping into her voice.

Kobolowski puffed his chest, relishing the moment.

"Police business, ma'am. If you could come with me, please?"

~

THE DOOR SWUNG OPEN, and Claire stepped into Muldoon's apartment. Her eyes widened in surprise as she took in the scene before her. The whole place had been magically transformed into what looked like a quaint Italian restaurant. A red-and-white checkered tablecloth covered a romantic dinner set for two, complete with candles flickering and dripping wax down old wine bottles. Colorful posters of Rome, Venice, and Florence decorated the walls.

Music began to play:

"Oh, this is the night, such a beautiful night, and they call it bella notte."

Claire's knees nearly buckled when Danny Muldoon walked into the room. He looked like he had just stepped off the cover of *GQ*—dressed in a perfectly tailored two-piece suit, a fitted shirt, and a crisp tie. His hair was styled with just the right amount of gel, not a strand out of place. Claire could feel her heart pounding in her chest, so loud she was sure he could hear it too.

"I did some recon on the flowers this time," he said, walking toward her, hiding something behind his back. With a mischievous grin, he extended his hand and revealed a huge bouquet of tulips—straight from Holland.

Claire threw her hands to her mouth in a gasp of pure delight.

"I figured, who needs Italy?" he said with a handsome smile. "This good, *right? Right?*"

She wiped away a tear and collected herself. "Danny, you know I wanted to let Andrew stay, but—"

"Shhhhh." He pressed a finger to her lips. "Talking is so overrated."

Then he pulled Claire close and kissed her—firm and passionate—making her heart race and her cheeks flush. Everything else seemed to fade away, and in that moment, nothing else in the whole world mattered.

SIX MONTHS LATER

Andrew and Claire sat in the front seat of her car, facing each other, eye to eye. A seriousness hung in the air as they both took a deep breath.

"You sure about this?" Andrew asked cautiously.

"Never been surer of anything in my life," Claire replied with confidence.

"I don't know," Andrew admitted hesitantly.

"Listen to me," Claire insisted. "You're going to be okay. I promise." She paused, then asked, "This is good, right?"

Andrew smiled back. "Right."

Claire clicked a colored pen and opened a unicorn notebook. "Alright. Proper forms are all in order," she said with mock authority.

"Look at you. So organized," Andrew replied with a grin. "Do me a favor and check in on Muldoon for me, will ya? Make sure he's not watching too much television."

"Roger that," Claire quipped, playfully mocking her new boyfriend.

Andrew hopped out of the car, closed the door, then leaned back in through the open window. "And you," he said, addressing someone in the back seat. "Make sure someone shows you around that new school. Like, where the cool kids sit and stuff. You're gonna want the right crew."

Ben, sitting buckled in the back with a name tag on, a dinosaur lunch box in hand, and his hair slicked back, replied, *"So long… partner."*

He was ready for school.

Claire glanced up at Mr. Wilden, who stood by the front door of the wood-shingled Cape house, waiting for Andrew. He looked better—more comfortable, more present—like the weight of the world had been lifted off his shoulders.

Claire smiled as she watched Andrew bounce out of the car and return home. His posture, his mannerisms, his overall demeanor—everything had changed. For a fleeting moment, he stopped being the teenager she once knew. Andrew was becoming a man. Happy. Confident. He belonged.

WILDEN HOUSE

Andrew and Molly settled onto the couch, the house around them now a picture of neatness, tidiness, and unexpected comfort. The usual piles of scattered tapes and DVDs had been completely cleared away. In their place was a space that felt strangely calm, almost serene, as if the very air had been scrubbed clean. It felt like a fresh start—quiet and hopeful.

Without a word, he dropped a book onto Molly's lap.

"Done."

"Did you read the whole thing? Every page?" she asked.

"You want me to quote a line," he replied, dripping with confidence.

Molly smiled.

Mr. Wilden stepped into the room, a noticeable change in his appearance. Gone was the familiar smock and bow tie, replaced by a soft plaid shirt and well-worn jeans. His shoulders, usually tense, were more relaxed, and his face carried a calmness that was new. It was as if shedding his old uniform had allowed him to finally embrace a version of himself he'd long forgotten—one that was more at ease, more genuine. The change made the whole house feel warmer, more inviting, like a space where everyone could finally breathe.

"Well, hello there, Molly. What are you two kids up to today?"

"Thought we'd watch a movie," Andrew replied.

His father frowned.

"Just this one. That's it," Andrew assured him.

"Well, okay," Mr. Wilden relented. Then, brimming with confidence, he announced, "I'm heading out to the park. It's a beautiful day. Get out and enjoy it. What time is your train?"

"Four-thirty," Andrew replied. "Mom is picking me up at Penn Station. I'll be back Sunday night."

"Not too late. You have school on Monday."

Father and son exchanged proud smiles before Mr. Wilden headed out of the house and into the world.

Andrew picked up the remote, then pointed it toward the TV. "Okay. You ready?"

Molly gently pushed the remote down.

"You know what? We watch movies when we want to escape," she said softly. "We don't have to do that anymore."

Andrew sat with that. Then—quietly—he set the remote aside.

The two teenagers leaned back together in comfortable silence, not escaping, not distracting, just being. Andrew looked toward the bay window—the same one he peered out of for years—but now, he was looking out into the world with confidence, not fear, finally ready to step into it.

In this moment, in this exact second, everything was perfect.

Bibliography

MOVIE LINES IN ORDER OF APPEARANCE:

"Get her. She's givin' out wings." – *It's a Wonderful Life*

"Good morning, dear. And in case I don't see ya, good afternoon, good evening, and good night!" – *The Truman Show*

"Don't mess with the bull, young man. You'll get the horns." – *The Breakfast Club*

"Bing!" – *Groundhog Day*

"Okay, campers, rise and shine, and don't forget your booties 'cause it's cooooold out there today. It's coooold out there every day." – *Groundhog Day*

"You come on down here and chum some of this sh…" – *Jaws*

"Saddle up. We're burning daylight!" – *The Cowboys*

"Come on, Dad. Dad. Dad. Dad, Dad, Dad." – *The Lion King*

"Eat. My. Shorts." – *The Breakfast Club*

"The athlete. The basket case. The princess. The criminal." – *The Breakfast Club*

"Hasta la vista, baby." – *The Terminator*

"You're gonna need a bigger boat." – *Jaws*

"Yes, I got a question. Does Barry Manilow know you raid his wardrobe?" – *The Breakfast Club*

"See this? This is this. This ain't something else. This is this." – *The Deer Hunter*

"You got any white bread?" – *The Blues Brothers*

"I'll have some toasted white bread, please." – *The Blues Brothers*

"We're on a mission from God." – *The Blues Brothers*

"Shall we play a game?" – *WarGames*

"You want jam on that dry white toast, honey?" – *The Blues Brothers*

"Just you and me. Two hits. Me hitting you. You hitting the floor." – *The Breakfast Club*

"Leave the gun. Take the cannoli." – *The Godfather*

"Arise, fair sun, and kill the envious moon, that thou, her maid, art far more fair than she." – *Romeo and Juliet*

"I was just gonna say—four o'clock." – *Ghostbusters*

"You're my density." – *Back to the Future*

"We're all pretty bizarre. Some of us are just better at hiding it, that's all." – *The Breakfast Club*

"You know, it's legal for me to take you down to the station and sweat it out of you under the lights." – *Dick Tracy*

"Juuuust a bit outside." – *Major League*

"You're killing me, Smalls. You're killing me!" – *The Sandlot*

Bibliography

"Pick me out a winner, Bobby." – *The Natural*

"There's no crying in baseball!" – *A League of Their Own*

"Hey batta hey batta batta batta SWING batta!" – *Ferris Bueller's Day Off*

"Serve the public, protect the innocent, uphold the law." – *RoboCop*

"Waiter, there is too much pepper on my paprikash." – *When Harry Met Sally*

"But I would be proud to partake of your pecan pie." – *When Harry Met Sally*

"There is no try. Only do." – *Return of the Jedi*

"Would you like to go to the movies with me tonight?" – *When Harry Met Sally*

"Life moves pretty fast. If you don't stop and look around once in a while, you could miss it." – *Ferris Bueller's Day Off*

"Eat me." – *Animal House*

"You gonna bark all day, little doggie...or are you gonna bite?" – *Reservoir Dogs*

"Hey bud, what's your problem?" – *Fast Times at Ridgemont High*

"You are a sad, strange little man. And you have my pity." – *Toy Story*

"Frankly, my dear, I don't give a damn." – *Gone with the Wind*

"I'm so cold, Jack." – *Titanic*

"Hold on tight, spider monkey." – *Twilight*

"Nobody puts Baby in a corner." – *Dirty Dancing*

"There's a new sheriff in town. Y'all be cool." – *48 Hours*

"You can be my wingman anytime." – *Top Gun*

"Just keep swimming." – *Finding Nemo*

"To infinity and beyond!" – *Toy Story*

"Aaaarrrrrggghh—Kelly Clarkson!" – *The 40-Year-Old Virgin*

"Grab a drink, don't cost nothin'." – *Animal House*

"Bring me a pitcher of beer every seven minutes until somebody passes out. Then bring one every ten minutes." – *Back to School*

"We're goin' streakin' in the quad!" – *Old School*

"I am a golden god!" – *Almost Famous*

"The first rule of Fight Club is: You do not talk about Fight Club." – *Fight Club*

"Say 'what' again. I dare you. I double dare you." – *Pulp Fiction*

"If done right... can no defense." – *The Karate Kid*

"There are a lot of things about me you don't know anything about. Things you wouldn't understand. Things you couldn't understand. Things you shouldn't understand." – *Pee-wee's Big Adventure*

"Mother? Mother, where are you?" – *Bambi*

"I have a feeling we're not in Kansas anymore." – *The Wizard of Oz*

"We are fighting for our right to live. To exist. We will not go quietly into the night! We will not vanish without a fight! We're going to live on! We're going to survive! Today we celebrate our Independence Day!" – *Independence Day*

"Would you be willing to trade ALL the days for one chance, just one chance, to tell our enemies that they may take our homework...but they'll never take...OUR FREEDOM!" – *Braveheart*

"Oh, this is the night, such a beautiful night, and they call it bella notte." – *Lady and the Tramp*

Bibliography

"Here you are. The best spaghetti and meatball in town." – *Lady and the Tramp*
"So long, partner." – *Toy Story 3*

This story was inspired by documentaries:

THE WOLF PACK – A coming-of-age story following the six Angulo brothers, who spent their entire lives locked away from society in an apartment on the Lower East Side of Manhattan. All they knew of the outside world came from the films they watched obsessively and recreated meticulously with homemade props and costumes. For years this served as a way to stave off loneliness — but when one of the brothers escaped, everything changed.

LIFE, ANIMATED – The inspirational story of Owen Suskind, a young man who was unable to speak as a child until he and his family discovered a way to communicate by immersing themselves in the world of classic Disney animated films.

About the Author

Mike Bernard is a multi-optioned screenwriter and the author of seven novels and a stage musical. His work has received international recognition in prestigious competitions, including the Academy Nicholl Fellowship, PAGE Awards, Big Break, and the screenplay contests in New York, Nantucket, and Los Angeles. His "midlife crisis" writing career began when both his children—and his money—went off to college.

Mike is a graduate of Providence College and Boston College High School. He lives on Cape Cod with his wife, Michele, where he spends his summers playing pickleball and his winters aimlessly roaming the aisles of Home Depot.